JOSIE'S BEAU

A RICHARD JACKSON BOOK

JOSIE'S BEAU

By Natalie Honeycutt

90/21

ORCHARD BOOKS

A DIVISION OF FRANKLIN WATTS, INC.
New York and London

Copyright © 1987 by Natalie Honeycutt

Orchard Books
387 Park Avenue South, New York, New York 10016

Orchard Books Great Britain
10 Golden Square, London W1R 3AF England

Orchard Books Australia
14 Mars Road, Lane Cove, New South Wales 2066

Orchard Books Canada
20 Torbay Road, Markham, Ontario 23P 1G6

Orchard Books is a division of Franklin Watts, Inc.

The text of this book is set in 12 pt. Janson.

Manufactured in the United States of America
Book design by Sylvia Frezzolini

10 9 8 7 6 5 4 3 2 1

Library of Congress Cataloging-in-Publication Data
Honeycutt, Natalie. Josie's Beau.
Summary: Josie's summer is busy as she tries to help her friend Beau
buy the skateboard of his dreams and they both have trouble from
a bullying peer. [1. Friendship—Fiction. 2. Bullies—Fiction]
I. Title.
PZ7.H7467Jo 1987 [Fic] 87-5732
ISBN 0-531-05718-6
ISBN 0-531-08318-7 (lib. bdg.)

For Judy,
best sister and best friend
_____

Chapter One

"This is dumb, Beau." Josie Pucinski watched as the back of yet another No. 38 Geary bus pulled away from the curb. It was the third that had left without them. "At this rate," she said, "we'll never get home."

"We'll get there," Beau said. He pulled a fat wallet out of his pocket and began leafing through its contents. "If only I had a light orange transfer. I thought I did, but I can't find it. Too bad today isn't a blue day. I have about a zillion blues."

"Well, you already looked, and you don't have one," Josie said. "There's no sense in looking again."

Beau had a large collection of discarded transfers, but he never had the right color on the right day. Josie didn't know why he bothered to save them. He shrugged and returned the wallet to his pocket. "That guy could have let me on the bus. I mean, look at it. That bus was nearly half a block long, and it had only five people on it. It wouldn't have killed the driver to let me on."

1

"He couldn't," Josie said. "Those are the rules. Nobody rides for free, and nobody rides with an invalid transfer. Maybe people ride for free in Detroit, or Atlanta for all I know, but nobody rides for free in San Francisco, Beau."

"Some people do," he said.

"Some *times* they do. But you're trying to ride for free all the time."

"It's not all the time," he said. "Sometimes we walk."

"*Mostly* we walk. That's the trouble. I wish you'd just buy a bus pass like a normal person."

"I can't," Beau said. "You know that."

"You just don't want to. That's different from *can't*."

"I can't, Josie. I need to save money for my skateboard."

Josie sighed. Beau's skateboard. All because of a skateboard he was convinced he couldn't live without, Beau had refused to buy a bus pass on the first of June. Instead, he had pocketed the money his mother gave him for the pass, and used it to make a payment on a skateboard deck. And now Josie was stuck with Beau's makeshift transportation arrangements.

Stick together, that was the deal. Their parents had had a big two-family conference in the spring, during which they had laid out the plans for the summer. And rule number one was "stick together when you're on the street."

2

"What are you going to do if your mother finds out you didn't buy a bus pass?" Josie asked. "Have you thought of that?"

"I can't worry about something that hasn't happened yet," Beau said. "Anyway, how would she find out? You're not going to tell her, are you?"

"Of course not! But she could figure it out if we keep getting home late."

"Come on, then," he said. "We'll have to walk."

"Beau! It's nearly twenty blocks!"

"Twenty-two to be exact. But look at it this way, Josie—it's good exercise."

Josie didn't need more exercise. She and Beau had just spent the entire afternoon walking around the San Francisco Zoo. What Josie needed now was a ride.

"If we walk, we're guaranteed to be late," Josie said. "I think our parents will figure out something's fishy. Aren't you worried about that?"

Beau shrugged. "Guess not," he said. He turned and began walking down Geary Boulevard toward home.

"Oh, no," Josie said. She rushed to catch up with him, then tried again. "Look, Beau . . . your mother is already steamed about Matt Ventura. Suppose she gets even madder?"

"That's different," Beau said. He didn't break stride. "She's upset because I've been fighting with Ventura. That doesn't have anything to do with when we get home."

3

Josie gave up. If fear of his mother wouldn't make Beau pay for a bus ride, nothing would.

Not that Paula Finch was the world's meanest mom. Far from it. It was just that she felt very strongly about some things, and when she felt strongly about things she sometimes got upset. When she got *very* upset, she sometimes yelled. Fighting was one of the things she felt strongly about.

"Anyway," Beau said, "it's not like I actually fight with Ventura. It's more like he fights and I lose. If my parents hadn't spent my whole life harping on how wrong violence is, I might *really* fight with him. And maybe I'd win, too. But fighting is his idea, not mine, so if there's anyone my mother should be mad at, it's Ventura, not me."

That was true, Josie had to admit. It was Matt Ventura who wanted to fight with Beau, not the other way around. So far as Josie knew, Beau Finch had never picked a fight with anyone in his life. And Josie would know—she and Beau had grown up together. He was not only her upstairs neighbor, but her oldest and best friend in the world.

The Finches and the Pucinskis had bought the building on 16th Avenue together when Josie and Beau were one year old, and the two families had shared much of their lives ever since—the Finches in the upper flat, the Pucinskis in the lower. They shared the mailbox, the backyard, the plumbing bills, Thanksgiving dinner, and anything else that came to mind.

And for eleven of their twelve years, Josie and Beau had shared growing up. They had learned to cross the street together, had gone to kindergarten and day care together, had learned to ride bikes at the same time, had even had chicken pox together. They were joint owners of an old red wagon, a rope swing, and a ramshackle structure under the backyard deck that was either a fort or a clubhouse, depending.

For a time, Josie remembered with some embarrassment, their parents had even bathed them together. She couldn't remember exactly how old they'd been when they'd had the baths, but it might have been around pre-school age. What she did remember was suddenly one day feeling extremely underdressed, and yelling at her mother that she would not take baths with that "silly boy" anymore, even if she got so dirty she had to live outside. No one had ever mentioned the baths again, including Beau. Sometimes Josie wondered whether he even remembered them, but she'd never had the courage to ask.

"You should explain to your mother that Matt Ventura starts the fights," Josie said. "Maybe then she'd understand."

"I've tried," Beau said. "But she keeps saying that it takes two people to fight, and that 'violence breeds violence.' I think she got that last part from one of those books she's always reading lately."

Josie could imagine Paula Finch saying that. Beau's

mother had recently quit her job and gone back to college to study sociology.

"I guess she hasn't gotten to the book that explains about people like Matt Ventura," Josie offered.

"There isn't a book that explains about people like Matt Ventura," Beau said. "I think he's just mean. I mean, you tell me, Josie—what has Ventura got against me, anyhow?"

"Well . . ." Josie said. Really she didn't know for certain, but if she had to guess . . . "I think he might be jealous because you're so popular."

"That's crazy," Beau said. "For one thing, I don't have any more friends than anyone else. And for another, who would care if I did?"

That was just like Beau, Josie thought. He was one of the world's most likeable people. And it wasn't even that there was something special about him to like. He was what most people would call average—average looks, average height, average intelligence, average wit. But he always assumed that people would like him. And inevitably they did.

Sometimes it annoyed Josie, especially when she felt she had to stand in line just to be his friend. But the worst was a day when Beau told her that some girl at Presidio Middle School had asked if Josie were his girlfriend. "I don't know why she'd think something stupid like that," Beau had said. "I told her we're just old friends. More like pals, really." That day Josie went home from school without him. And when he rang her doorbell later and asked why, she only said, "Because sometimes I get sick of talking to you."

But if Beau Finch didn't know or care that he was popular, Josie had the idea that Matt Ventura did. And that he didn't like it.

"Do you remember the day Matt came to school with that snake tattooed on his upper arm?" Josie asked. They had just crossed 20th Avenue, and Beau was walking a little faster.

"Yeah! That was really strange," Beau said.

"I don't think you should have *said* it was strange, though. I don't think Matt appreciated it."

"What should I have said, then—'Hey, that's cool'? I mean it *is* strange to get a tattoo in sixth grade, Josie. I thought that was for older guys. Like bikers."

"Even so, it would have been better if you hadn't said anything. Because as soon as you said it, the kids who were hanging around looking at Matt's tattoo started to leave. Then Kristy Kesler began giggling, and she followed you to your locker."

"Kristy is like that. She hangs around and giggles all the time. It drives me nuts."

Me too, Josie thought. "But Matt likes her," she said. She didn't bother to mention that most of the other boys at school liked her, too.

"So?"

"Good grief, Beau. Don't you understand anything? It was the next day that Matt Ventura tripped you on the stairs."

"And the week after that he dropped my math book in the toilet."

"Exactly. And the next week he punched you in the stomach," Josie said.

"Well, for crying out loud!" Beau said. "I wish he'd *told* me he was mad that I didn't like his tattoo. I could have said I liked it, and then none of these fights would have happened, and my mother wouldn't be on my case." He kicked at a discarded paper cup in his path. "If that's all that's bothering him, I'll tell him I think his tattoo is cool. I can tell him on Monday, in fact, when we see him at swimming."

"I don't think that will work, Beau."

"Sure it will," Beau said. "It's easy. You'll see."

Beau was walking very fast now, and Josie had to run every few steps to keep up. "It's just not as simple as saying his tattoo is cool." She shook her head. "Really, Beau, sometimes I don't understand how you get good grades in school."

"I study."

"You must," she said. "Very hard."

Beau broke into a trot, and Josie jogged along after him for a few yards. Then she stopped. She was exhausted, out of breath, and her feet hurt. Beau continued down the street, oblivious.

"Beau Finch," she yelled. "You creep, wait up!" She ran again to overtake him. "First we have to walk about a thousand miles, and then you start running. Jeez. I mean, if we're not even going to walk together, I might as well use my bus pass and ride home."

"Sorry. I thought you were with me, Josie, I really did." He gave her a sheepish grin. "It's just that if we hurry, I thought we could stop by Skeet's Skates on the way home and visit my board."

"Beau!" Josie said. "Skeet's Skates is not on the way home. It's all the way over on Clement Street. That's ten blocks out of our way!"

"Twenty," Beau said. "Round trip."

"Forget it, Beau. I've walked enough for one day. And besides, we just visited your skateboard on Tuesday, if you remember. I'm sure it hasn't changed any."

"Of course it hasn't changed," Beau said. "That's not the point. I just like to look at it sometimes. And make sure they don't sell it to someone else."

Josie sighed. "They wouldn't do that, Beau. You put a deposit on it, and they can't sell it to someone else."

"Well . . ." Beau said. They crossed 17th Avenue. "I know they wouldn't, really. But sometimes I wonder. Like if somebody really rich came in and saw what a rad board it is and offered Skeet double the usual price, then he might sell it."

"That couldn't happen, Beau."

"Yeah, but you can't be sure."

Josie was sure. She was sure that nobody in the world except Beau Finch would be making payments on a fifty-dollar skateboard deck that didn't even

9

have wheels yet. *Nobody* would pay double for it—especially considering that it was ugly: black with a purple heart on the bottom with a dagger sticking through it. The dagger dripped blood.

"I'm sure enough," Josie said. "Take a chance; forget your skateboard for today. Besides, I'm tired."

"You could rest when we get home," Beau coaxed.

"No!" Josie was getting fed up. "I'm not walking another foot today, especially not for your skateboard. Plus, we're almost late now. We'll be really late if we go to Clement Street. And then you know what could happen."

"Yeah," Beau laughed. "Your mother will decide we've been abducted, so she'll call my mother. Then my mother will dial 911 and make a Missing Children report. By dinner time they'd have our pictures on nine million milk cartons."

Josie laughed in spite of herself. "You're hopeless," she said. "I *meant* that if we're late your mother might figure out why." They rounded the corner onto 16th Avenue. "I just wish you'd buy a bus pass like everyone else, Beau. I don't think I can stand a whole summer of these forced marches."

"But what about my skateboard?" Beau asked.

"You could find another way to make money."

"I tried the *Chronicle*," Beau said. "They say they have a waiting list of people who want to deliver papers in our neighborhood. It could be years before my name comes up."

"Then try something else," Josie said. "There must be another way. I could even help you think of some ideas. I'm sure I could come up with a list."

"Okay, I'll consider it."

"Do," Josie said. "It's either that or buy me new feet."

Beau laughed. "Okay, okay. Boy, you're really stubborn, Josie Pucinski, you know that?"

"I know," Josie said. She grinned as they tromped up the front steps of their building. "It's one of my very best qualities."

Chapter Two

Josie ran her hand around the bottom of the kitchen sink, under the suds, feeling for stray silverware. She found a fork, rinsed it under the faucet, and popped it in the drainer.

Her mother, still in the uniform she wore for her job as a laboratory technician, stood at the counter unpacking a bag of groceries.

"Done," Josie announced. She pulled the plug from the sink and watched as the water burbled down the drain. "I absolutely hate dishes. They're so boring."

"Tell me about it," Sandy Pucinski said. She reached around Josie to put a roll of paper towels on the rack.

"The worst part is that it takes forever," Josie said.

"No, that part's merely bad. The worst part is that there will be another big pile of them right after dinner."

"Ugh. Don't remind me."

"And tomorrow, and the next day, and the next."

"Stop," Josie said. "You're making me miss Kim. When it's her turn to do the dishes, I start *longing* for her to get home from camp."

"Josie, you don't know when you're well off," her mother said. "As sisters go, Kim is one of the good kind."

"I *know* she is," Josie said. She felt at a loss to explain herself. Kim was pretty, talented at music, had lots of friends and a steady stream of boyfriends. She was usually even nice to Josie, or had been in recent years. So it wasn't that there was really anything wrong with Kim at all. It was just that it was nice to have her *gone* sometimes.

With Kim away at music camp, the elder Pucinskis "discovered" Josie. They remembered to ask her how her day was, talked to her as though she was older than three, and consulted her about what to have for dinner. Sometimes Josie wished she were an only child.

Of course, some of the discoveries her parents made were *un*pleasant. Last summer, for instance, Josie's parents discovered that Josie had received a D in spelling for the year, so they made her do exercises in a spelling book every day of the three weeks that Kim was away. Then, when Kim got home from camp, they forgot about it. The trick, Josie decided, was to help guide their discoveries into pleasant areas whenever possible.

"Tell you what," her mother said. "I'm going to

give you another chance to miss Kim. You can wash the lettuce for me—that's usually Kim's job."

"Never mind," Josie said. "I think I miss her enough already. Besides, I have something to do in my room."

"Like clean it, I hope," her mother called after her.

Josie pretended she hadn't heard. She wanted to start her list of ways for Beau to earn money. She was sure to think of things that he wouldn't.

Josie walked down the long hall to the back of the flat. As she passed the open door to Kim's room, she glanced in. It was so big, so spacious. So *neat*. Kim's bear was propped against the pillows on her bed, cosmetics and perfumes were in careful rows on her bureau, and books and stationery boxes were stacked evenly on her desk. Hanging over Kim's bed was a large poster advertising a concert by Yo-Yo Ma, a famous cellist. There was something so orderly and quiet about the room that it somehow felt like a shrine. A shrine to Kim, Josie thought.

She walked in and stood in front of Kim's desk. In the center of it was a pile of college catalogs Kim had begun collecting over the spring and summer. This fall she would be applying to colleges, and a year from now she would be getting ready to go.

Josie leafed through the pile: New England Conservatory, Eastman School of Music, Oberlin Conservatory, and Indiana University. There was even one from the Juilliard School of Music, a place Josie had chiefly heard mentioned as a school Kim probably couldn't get into. But Kim said it didn't hurt to send for their catalog. She not only had always believed she'd go to college and major in music, she assumed it.

Josie's father said nearly everyone was talented in something and the trick was to recognize it. He prided himself on having recognized Kim's talent early and having helped her get started on the cello. But Josie had proved a tougher case. No one had yet figured out what her talent was, if indeed she had one at all, which Josie had begun to doubt. Clearly it wasn't music. After two years of flute lessons, even Josie could tell that she didn't have an especially good ear. And it wasn't art either; Josie could see the difference between her drawings and those of, say, Beau, who could draw anything and make it look three-dimensional. And it wasn't sports. Josie was persistently average at anything athletic.

Josie figured if she had to wait until she was grown up for her talent to appear, she wasn't interested in it. After all, by then she would presumably have learned to live without one.

She left Kim's room and walked through her parents' bedroom to her own small room at the back of the flat.

"Ugh," she said. There was no denying that it did need to be cleaned. It needed so much cleaning, in fact, that Josie wasn't sure she was up to the job. She sank to the edge of the bed and looked around hopelessly.

One of the problems was that it wasn't a proper

bedroom at all. It was actually a sunroom, with doors that opened both into Kim's room and into her parents'. And it was a room without a closet, so the few dresses Josie owned usually hung in Kim's closet.

Still, closets were for more than hanging things in, and Josie felt she could have used one. Much of the stuff that littered the floor and surfaces of the room could be safely shoved into a closet, and the room would be clean almost instantly.

Maybe if she threw a few things out . . . But what? Surely not her dolls. Josie no longer played with them, but one just didn't throw out faithful old dolls simply because the time for them was past. Or her stuffed animals. She no longer felt the need to sleep with all twenty-three, but there was no space for them other than on her bed.

Well, if she couldn't clean her room, maybe she could improve it just a bit before she began her list for Beau. Josie began gathering the dirty clothes that were littered about. That would make a difference.

She made small piles of socks and underwear and slacks. A sweater she folded and crammed into the large bureau that blocked the door to Kim's room.

Why was it that dirty clothes looked so much more worn out than clean ones did? These struck Josie as mostly worn out. Or outgrown. Like this green print shirt. She held it up to her chest, flopped a sleeve out along one arm, and looked in the mirror. And she'd worn it only three days ago! Why hadn't someone mentioned to her how silly it looked for her bony wrists to be hanging inches below the cuff?

And it was green besides. Kim's color. One of the things Josie disliked most about getting hand-me-downs from Kim was the endless green. Green looked fine on Kim, who had green eyes. But Josie had blue eyes, and anyone could see that green was simply putrid on her.

She collected the pile of dirty clothes, keeping the green patterned shirt separate in her hand, and marched to the front of the flat. She could help her parents "discover" that her clothes were too small, since they seemed unable to do it on their own.

Josie's father was home. His coat and tie were off, and he was standing at the sink washing the lettuce. "Hi, peaches," he said as she went past him to the utility room.

Josie dumped the laundry in the hamper and came back to stand in front of her father, the offensive shirt still in her hand.

"I have a complaint," she said.

"No 'hello' first?" He grinned.

"Hello. My complaint is that I'm outgrowing all of my clothes and nobody seems to care. Nobody even *noticed*. Look," she said accusingly, and held the green shirt up in front of her.

Bill Pucinski stroked his chin. "Hmmm . . ." he said.

"The wrists," Josie said. "Look at my wrists. They stick out."

"Hmmm . . ." he said again. "So they do."

Her mother left the stove to stand next to him. She eyed Josie and the shirt carefully. "Oh, my," she said. "When did that happen?"

"Some time last year, by the look of things," her father said. He seemed amused.

"So what are you going to do about it?" Josie asked. "I think they're all like this—my clothes."

"Well," Sandy Pucinski said, "the usual, I guess. As soon as Kim gets back, we'll have her sort through her clothes to see what she's outgrown."

"Not so fast," Bill Pucinski said. "I think we have an unforeseen problem." He took Josie by the shoulder and steered her to the kitchen door jamb against which her own and Kim's heights had been marked off over the years. "Wait here," he said.

There was Josie's mark of last September. Height five feet, two inches; age, eleven and a half. And there was Kim's of the same day: age, sixteen and a half; height, five feet, five and a half inches.

Bill Pucinski returned with a stiff book, a pencil, and a ruler. He handed the ruler to Josie, then leveled the book on her head and made a careful line under it.

"Aha!" he said. "There it is in black and white. Go ahead and measure it, Josie."

Josie gaped. It couldn't be possible. Her new mark was more than an inch and a quarter above Kim's. Josie was pushing five feet, seven inches. She measured it again, just to be sure. It was the same.

"Oh, no . . ." she murmured.

"I can't believe my eyes," her mother said.

"Congratulations!" Bill Pucinski thumped Josie on the back.

"You mean 'deepest sympathy,' " Josie said. "How would *you* like to be the tallest person in the whole universe?"

"I'm six-three," her father said, "so you're not even close."

"But I'm taller than everyone my age," Josie said. "That's what counts. I was the tallest girl in my grade even before school was out. Think what it's going to be like when I go back!"

"Well, they'll be growing, too," her mother said.

Josie snorted. "Let them grow. They'll never catch up now. And the boys. Didn't anyone ever tell you that boys don't like tall girls?"

"I like your mother, and she's tall," Bill Pucinski said. "Besides, by the time you're old enough to be interested in boys, there'll be some as tall as you."

That was just like Josie's father. He thought you should be twenty years old to be interested in boys. "Wrong," Josie said. "I mean, what if I get interested in boys next year?" Or next month, she thought. Or yesterday?

"If you're thinking of Beau," her mother said, "don't worry. He'll grow."

Josie felt her cheeks grow warm. "Who said I was talking about Beau?" she asked. "Anyway, what makes you so sure he'll grow? Not that I care . . ."

19

"If you just look at his father, you'll see," her mother said. "Marc Finch is very tall, and Beau is built just like him. He'll get there."

Josie would have a hard time looking at Beau's father, even if she had wanted to. A biologist who ordinarily worked at the University of California, Marc Finch was presently in Central America discovering new species of trees. He had been there for three months already. Josie scanned her memory, trying to get a picture of him that looked like Beau. All she could get was that Beau was short and his father was tall.

"Beau's mother is short," she said. "Kids can take after either parent, right?"

"Yes, but Beau isn't *built* like his mother. Paula Finch has large bones. Beau is slight, like his father," Sandy Pucinski said. Then she went on, "I'll tell you what, Josie—I *promise* you that Beau Finch will tower over you someday. It's an absolute guarantee. How's that?"

Josie's cheeks were hot now. "It doesn't matter to me," she said. "He can stay shrimpy for the rest of his life if he wants to. It's not like he's my boyfriend or anything."

"I'm relieved to hear it," her father said. "Now let's resolve this problem with the clothes."

"Well, Kim has lots . . ." Josie began. Then she realized what her father had meant by an unforeseen problem. "Good grief! They won't fit me. Kim's hand-me-downs won't fit me anymore."

20

"Right!" her father said.

"Yow!" Josie whooped. "I'm free! No more green! You guys have finally discovered something about me that I actually like."

Her mother groaned. "I can't say that *I* like it," she said. "It looks as though we're going to have to provide you with a wardrobe of your own. Unless we can find someone taller than five-seven who can pass things on to you." She turned to her husband. "Do we know any girls taller than five-seven, Bill?"

"Just you," he said.

"Oh no, she can't have *my* clothes," Josie's mother said.

"Well then"—Bill Pucinski grinned at Josie—"looks like you're going shopping, Stretch."

Josie ignored the "Stretch" and ran for the door. "Call me when dinner's ready," she said. "I have a list to make."

She cleared a space, sat at her desk, and pulled out some binder paper. Actually, it was two lists now—one of all the new clothes she would need, and the other for Beau. She began with Beau's.

Ways To Make Money
1. Sell vitamins door-to-door.

If Beau sold vitamins door-to-door, Josie reasoned, he might start taking them. And if he started taking them, he might grow.

Chapter Three

Beau checked his watch. "Ten minutes of," he said to Josie. "We're just barely going to make it." They were walking down Anza Street to Rossi Pool.

Josie waited for Beau to complain that it had taken her too long to gather up her swimming gear that morning. When he did, she would be ready for him. She'd remind him that if they had taken the bus instead of walking, they'd be early. But Beau didn't say anything further. Maybe he was learning.

"So what did you think of the list?" Josie asked.

"What list?"

"The list of ways to earn money for your skateboard. You did read it, didn't you?"

"Oh, yeah," Beau said. "It was good. Except for the idea of renting myself out to people who are thinking of having kids but want to try it out first. I don't think my mother would go for that one."

"What about the rest, then? Like pet-sitting. Or washing cars. You could do one of those, Beau."

"I think I probably can't make enough money just pet-sitting or washing cars," Beau said. "So I thought maybe I'd do a little bit of everything. I can haul people's trash cans out on garbage night, do yard work, return overdue books to the library for a fee, wash cars—all of that. Then I could really make some money. I think I'll advertise my*self*, see. Like 'Beau's Super Services.' Something like that."

"Only be sure to say 'Reasonable Rates,' " Josie offered. "I think a lot of people charge very unreasonable rates, and that's why they don't get any jobs." They stopped at Arguello Boulevard and waited for the light to change.

"Okay. And this afternoon we'll make the flyers and take them around."

"Flyers?" Josie said. "And 'we'? I thought you were the one who was going to get a job. Plus, we were going to Fisherman's Wharf today, weren't we?"

"I have to advertise, Josie; otherwise nobody will know they can hire me. And I thought you'd want to help. But of course if you'd rather go to Fisherman's Wharf alone . . ."

"No," Josie said. "I'll help. That's okay. I *could* think of a couple of better ways to spend the afternoon, but I'll help if you want." She sighed. It would be a whole lot more convenient if Beau would yearn for something cheap. Like a bag of marbles. She could buy those for him herself.

23

They ran up the steps to Rossi Pool, gave the woman behind the window their quarters, and headed for the locker rooms.

There were several things Josie didn't like about these swimming lessons. One of them was standing around waiting for her class's turn to get into the water. She always felt as though people were staring at her. Not that they were, but there was always the possibility that they might. And Josie was fairly sure she looked silly in her Speedo bathing suit. First there were her long, skinny, stalklike legs; then everything else just went straight up and down—except for the bumps where her chest was finally beginning to develop. Those were probably the most noticeable of all. Josie wasn't sure whether people would notice them chiefly for their small size or because they were there in the first place, but she was sure they called attention to themselves in some way.

On days when they were early to swimming class, Josie spent the waiting time doing a good imitation of being very cold so that she would have a reason to huddle her arms around herself. But today she arrived at poolside just as the whistle blew to signal her class into the water.

Josie hopped in at the four-foot depth and looked around for Beau. He came up on her left side.

"If Ventura tries to drown me again, call the lifeguard or something," Beau said.

Josie checked down the row of kids for Matt. He

was third down on her right. Last week he had been in the lane next to Beau and had yanked Beau under the water in a sneak attack.

"I think you're safe," Josie said. "There are three people between the two of you. He'd have to really go out of his way to drown you."

"Yeah, but keep your eyes open anyhow, okay?" Beau said. "I think he's highly motivated."

"Kick!" Don yelled. Don was the swimming teacher, and he was the second thing Josie disliked about these lessons. During the first session of swimming lessons, Josie and Beau had been assigned to Cathy, who had learned everyone's name right away, and by the end of two weeks had taught everyone the crawl stroke. Even the "hopeless cases" like Josie, who couldn't so much as float on the first day, had learned the crawl. Cathy was good.

Don was something else. He was a hulking guy whose mouth hung slack except when he was shouting orders. His way of teaching swimming was to tell everyone to kick, then he'd count to fifteen. Next he'd yell "Breathe!" and count to fifteen again while everyone practiced rhythmic breathing at the side of the pool. Finally he would yell, "Okay, everyone swim laps!" and for the rest of the thirty-minute lesson you had to swim laps back and forth across the pool. That was it, his whole thing. It was pretty stupid, Josie thought. And it also sort of fit with Don, if you looked at the expression on his face.

25

"Breathe!" Don yelled. "One, two, three, four, five, six . . ."

Josie shook her head and started the breathing.

"Fifteen! Okay, everyone swim laps. Go!"

Whatever they were supposed to learn from this method wasn't working for Josie. She felt she was becoming a worse swimmer every day, not a better one. She plunged into the water and began stroking hard. The girl to Josie's right kicked off just after Josie, and in a few seconds had passed her. On the other side, Beau's foot splash was getting in Josie's face.

Josie stood up and rubbed the water out of her eyes. Everyone in her class had nearly reached the other side of the pool. Josie had made it exactly one third of the way. She leaped forward and began to swim harder, then stopped to rest again when her strength gave out. In a few seconds the other kids in the class began to pass Josie going the other way.

"I'm lousy at this," she said to no one in particular. It was so frustrating. Useless, really. She would never be a decent swimmer, and Don was no help.

Doggedly, Josie continued her laps for another ten minutes. She lost count of how many times the other kids passed her going either direction.

Josie checked the wall clock. Ten minutes of this stuff still to go. She was ready for home right now. She wondered what would happen if she just left the pool. Would anyone try to stop her? Would Don yell at her to get back in the water and kick?

She decided to walk. Not home, but across the pool. She kept moving her arms as though she were swimming, but instead of kicking Josie walked. Since she had such long legs, she figured she might as well use them.

Suddenly someone swam into her from the side. "Watch out," Josie said. Jeez. She didn't know which was worse, herself walking or someone else swimming crosswise to the traffic.

A snake writhed on the shoulder of the swimmer who had bumped her. Matt Ventura! And he was heading toward Beau! What should she do? Beau wasn't actually drowning yet. Josie couldn't very well yell that Beau was drowning when he wasn't.

"*Shark!*" Josie screamed. "Look out! Shark! *Shark!*" She stood screaming and pointing at Matt.

One by one the other kids in the pool stopped swimming and turned to see what was happening. Beau stopped, and even Matt stood up and began looking around in a bewildered way.

Don had been standing with his back to the pool, talking with a lifeguard. But at a gesture from the lifeguard, he too turned around.

"Hey" he bellowed. "What's going on here? Laps! You're supposed to swim laps!"

"*Shark!*" Josie screamed, pointing at Matt.

"Hey you!" Don yelled. He was pointing at Matt. "Get back where you belong. We're swimming laps here. No fooling around."

Matt seemed uncertain. "Who, me?" he asked, pointing to himself.

"Yes, *you*!" Don yelled. "Back in your lane!" Then he pointed at Josie. "And you! No more games!"

Matt shrugged and began a slow paddle back to his lane. As he passed Josie, he gave her a puzzled look. Josie stuck out her tongue. Then she turned to smile at Beau, who flashed her a thumbs-up.

When the whistle blew, Josie hauled herself out of the pool and walked stiff-legged and shivering to the women's locker room. She was always cold by the end of a lesson and eager to get into dry clothes.

She dried hurriedly. Not only was she anxious to be dressed and warm, but inevitably Beau dressed more quickly and was waiting on the sidewalk outside Rossi Pool when Josie got there.

She arrived breathless and still chilled. Beau was nowhere in sight. Some sun would help, Josie thought. But sun in the Richmond District in summertime, as her mother always said, was as rare as fog in the desert. Josie waited in fog.

She pulled up the hood of her sweatshirt. Beau was taking forever. What could he be doing? Maybe he had lost something. A sock. Or his locker. Josie began to pace.

Matt Ventura came by, running. He shot Josie a look but didn't slow down. Other kids came by at intervals of a minute or so, but still no Beau.

Josie jumped around, trying to get warm. She couldn't wait until Beau arrived. It wasn't just that she was anxious to leave, but she was beginning to think what a good opportunity this would be to razz him for being late. She imagined it in her head: "Boy, are you ever slow. I've been out here hours, freezing to death, waiting for you. And you complain about *me*! What happened, did you lose your way?" It would be delicious.

Then Beau arrived. His face was blotchy, contrasts of red and white, and a small trickle of blood ran from his nose.

"Beau! What happened?" Josie was alarmed.

Beau walked past her. "Let's get out of here," he said.

"But what *happened*? Beau, your nose is bleeding."

"Is it?" Beau wiped his sleeve across his face, smearing blood over the blue and white stripes of the shirt. "Great," he said. "Now I've wrecked my shirt, too. It was Ventura. I don't know what's wrong with him, Josie. All I said was, 'Hey, Ventura, I've been meaning to tell you how cool your tattoo is.' But instead of being happy, he says, 'Nobody asked you, Finch!' and shoves my face into a locker."

"Good grief," Josie said. She felt an impulse to do something to help, but Beau was walking with such determination that keeping up was as much as she could manage. She looked at the blood smeared on his sleeve and at the continuing trickle from one

29

nostril. It made her queasy. The sight of her own blood never bothered her, but somehow the sight of someone else's was faintly sickening. Beau's was even worse. "Did you tell someone?" she asked.

"Well, Don came in. But he didn't seem too interested, especially since Ventura explained that it was an accident."

"Don's dumb," Josie said. "Matt Ventura should be banned from the pool."

Beau shrugged. "It's no big deal," he said.

Josie took that as Beau's signal that he didn't want to talk about it any longer, so she walked along with him in silence. Every few seconds she stole a look at him. There was something familiar about that blotchy look to his face. . . .

Then it came to her. Beau's face always got blotchy when he cried. He'd been crying. She felt another surge of sympathy for him. Beau would almost rather die than have anyone see him cry. This was hard for Josie to understand; if she got hurt, she was more than happy to have everyone know it. And people certainly knew it if you also happened to be crying, preferably loudly. But Beau had become weird about crying in the last few years. He acted as though it was something he should have outgrown, like playing with blocks.

Well, if Beau didn't want her to know he'd been crying, Josie wouldn't bring it up.

"Do you want to go visit your skateboard?" she asked. That would make him feel better.

"I was just thinking of that," Beau said. His mouth twitched up in the beginning of a smile.

They turned north, crossed Geary Boulevard, and turned west again on Clement Street, one of the few streets where Josie would rather walk than ride. The clutter of small shops that lined both sides of it was endlessly fascinating to her.

Some were old stores, like Woolworth's, which for years Josie's mother had been predicting would go out of business. Now even Josie couldn't pass by without saying, "What do you know, Woolworth's is still here!"

Then there were the newer shops, many of which had an unsettling way of turning from shoe stores into restaurants or baby boutiques and then back into fancier shoe stores, all within the space of a few months. It was confusing, but also challenging. Josie liked to stand in front of a new flower shop and try to guess what had been there last week.

Best, though, were the heavy smells of Chinese cooking that hung like little oases across the sidewalk. Josie's mouth would start to water before she'd walked three blocks.

Skeet's Skates was one of the newer stores on the street, and because it was always crowded, Josie was betting it would last. The sign on the window said Skeet's Skates in large, Day-Glo script, and right underneath, Joseph "Skeet" Robertson, Proprietor.

Beau stood at the counter between boys who were examining wheels and brake pads. He didn't mind waiting. This was the part that bored Josie most. Beau would be perfectly content to stand for hours waiting his turn, leafing through the latest issue of *Thrasher* magazine.

It was Josie's impression that one issue of *Thrasher* was exactly like the next, so usually she sat in one of the two chairs and just watched the customers or tried to decide which of the hundreds of skateboard decks that lined the walls she would buy if she wanted a skateboard, which she didn't.

Today, though, Josie stood next to Beau and tried to look interested as he explained the virtues of the various brands of trucks that were advertised in the magazine.

Finally Skeet approached them. "Hi, Beau," he said. "Are you here to make a payment, or just visiting?"

"Both," Beau said. He pulled two dollars out of his pocket and put it on the counter. His allowance.

Skeet picked up a notebook from beside the cash register, flipped through several pages and began writing. "Two dollars on June eighteenth," he said, "leaving you a balance of fifteen dollars on the deck itself, plus whatever for accessories. You're getting there, Beau."

"Slowly but surely," Beau said. "May I see my board now?"

"Sure thing." Skeet flipped the notebook shut and disappeared into a back room, returning a moment later with Beau's board. He put it on the counter in front of Beau, then turned his attention to another customer.

"Wow," Beau said, just as though he had never seen it before. He always said "wow" when he saw it, which made Josie a little nervous. She was afraid that if he ever got to take it home, the skateboard would keep him awake nights.

"Isn't it a beauty, Josie?"

"Sure," Josie said. She had this part all worked out. Her father always said that beauty was in the eye of the beholder, so Josie figured that as long as Beau was the beholder, the skateboard was definitely beautiful. It didn't matter so much then that she herself couldn't imagine why anyone would want a skateboard with such a gory design on it. It struck Josie as menacing, though it was on the bottom where nobody could possibly see it anyhow.

Beau had explained to Josie that the design had to be on the bottom because friction pads for your feet went on top. But it worried Josie that Beau was paying extra for a design that nobody would ever see.

"I'm beginning to think Day-Glo green wheels on this would look really rad," Beau said.

Josie stifled an "ick." Beau's plans for the deck's accessories changed every week. With any luck, when he finally had money to buy wheels, he'd be in a yellow or red week.

Beau turned the board over, top side up, and began

buffing off fingerprints with the edge of his shirt sleeve.

Josie rolled her eyes. "Careful you don't get blood on it," she said.

Beau jumped. "Oh! Thanks, Josie." He pulled out the tail of his shirt and began buffing with that.

Josie regretted mentioning the blood. It was intended as a joke, but there was really no joking with Beau where his skateboard was concerned. Josie began to feel restless.

Skeet stopped in front of Beau again. "What do you think?" he asked. "Is it still the deck you want, or would you like to pick out a less expensive model?"

"No!" Beau said. "I mean yes. This is it. This is the deck I want. You won't sell it to someone else, will you?"

Skeet laughed. "No, not as long as you still want it."

"Oh, I want it all right. And I won't change my mind, either, so remember that."

"Tell you what," Skeet said. "I'll just slap one of these stickers on it, and that way I'll remember—in case I get tempted." He pulled out a red-and-black Sold sticker and stuck it to the top of the board.

"Thanks," Beau said. He sounded genuinely relieved.

Two blocks down from Skeet's Skates, Josie stopped in front of a dim sum shop. Her desire for Chinese food was overwhelming.

"Would you like a bean cake?" she asked Beau.

"Can't," he said. "I'm broke."

"But do you *want* one? I already know you're broke."

"Well . . . yeah."

"That's what I thought," Josie said. "I'll buy." She didn't mind spending her allowance on treats for both of them. Treats were better if they were shared, and that was what an allowance was for, she reasoned—to spend. She supposed she would feel differently if she were saving up for something, but it had been ages since she had wanted anything enough to save for it.

She bought two pork-stuffed bean cakes at the dim sum shop, then they continued walking west as they ate.

Suddenly Beau stopped. "You know, maybe it wasn't such a good idea to let Skeet put that tag on my board," he said.

"Oh, Beau, now what? I thought that was what you wanted—to make sure it wouldn't be sold to someone else by accident."

"Yeah, but the gum on the back of that tag . . . I'm afraid it might damage the paint when we try to take it off."

"*Beau*," Josie said. "You're really a case. What are you going to do with that skateboard when you get it, anyhow?"

"Ride it, of course," Beau said.

"Like outside?" Josie asked.

"Sure."

"On the sidewalks?"

"Yeah."

"Over *curbs*?"

"Naturally."

"In Golden Gate Park on Sundays?"

"Of *course*," Beau said.

"Well, I don't think that's such a good idea, Beau," Josie said solemnly.

"Why not? What's with you, Josie? What good is a skateboard if you can't ride it?"

"But Beau . . ." Josie paused, then used her most sugary voice. "It might get a . . . scratch!"

Beau narrowed his eyes and studied Josie for a second. Then he tore off a small piece of his bean cake and chucked it at her. "You don't understand," he said.

"Sure I do," Josie laughed. "You're going to have to build a glass case to keep that skateboard in when you get it home."

Beau chucked another piece of bean cake at her.

"Or a whole museum," Josie laughed, dancing away.

"I'm going to get you," Beau said.

Josie took off at a run. "Good thing it isn't a girl," she yelled. "You'd probably kiss it!"

"And when I get you, I'm going to rub bean cake all over your face," Beau called, pounding after her. "I'm going to cream you, Josie Pucinski!"

Chapter Four

Josie woke on Saturday morning feeling she'd slept late. It was hard to tell for sure because the thick fog outside her windows made it impossible to tell where the sun might be. Still, even on a foggy day the morning sounded different at nine than at six, and this morning's sound was definitely late.

She rolled onto her back and stared at the ceiling. There was no noise in Beau's room above hers. That proved it. Beau never slept late, so if his room was quiet it was probably because he had dressed and left it already. Maybe he had gone out to deliver those flyers. Josie had agreed to help Beau distribute them this morning, but it wouldn't break her heart if he'd decided not to wait for her.

She stretched the fingers on her right hand and massaged the palm. All those flyers. You wouldn't believe how sore your hand could get after writing "baby-sitting" and "yard work" one hundred and fifty times.

To top it all off, Beau had written "resonable" on every single flyer. When Josie had pointed it out, Beau just said, "I don't think people who want their cars washed will care whether or not I can spell." Josie only hoped he was right.

She moved her tongue around in her mouth. She had two loose teeth on the bottom. Molars. They weren't loose enough to come out yet, but they were getting tender. That was usually a good sign.

There was a light tap on her door, and her mother walked in. She looked at the array of junk lying about the floor and frowned slightly.

"I'm glad you're up," she said. "Your father and I have to leave soon."

"Oh," Josie said, remembering. Her parents were driving to Carmel Valley to pick up Kim at music camp.

"It's not too late to change your mind if you'd like to come along," her mother said.

"No, that's okay. I'd rather hang out with Beau." Josie had taken the trip with her parents to pick up Kim the previous year and had decided that it was one of those things that wasn't especially exciting unless you happened to be Kim. All Josie got out of it was a long car ride, a long concert, the chance to see teenagers hug one another good-bye, and then another long car ride home. All this while Kim monopolized her parents' attention. It was a good day for Josie to stay home.

"Get moving then," her mother said. "Paula is expecting you upstairs. She'll feed you dinner with Beau, and you can spend the night there."

"Oh, neat!"

"But hustle, Josie. I'd like you to be ready to leave when we are."

It was mysterious to Josie why her parents let her stay alone in the flat sometimes and not other times. It made sense at night because being alone at night was slightly scary, even with the Finches just upstairs. But it seemed to Josie that whether her parents were at work or a hundred miles away, one daytime was much like another. There ought to be a law, she thought, that your parents could only make you do things that made sense. But grown-ups, who had all the votes, would never vote for such a law. It was disheartening.

Josie stuck a finger in her mouth and wiggled one of the loose molars. If she worked at it, she might get it out by tonight. Then she could be paid for it tomorrow—though even the Tooth Fairy was a system that was stacked against kids. Josie knew from hard experience.

In her family they didn't have a Tooth Fairy at all any more. Instead, they had a Tooth Prince. More like the Prince of Darkness, Josie thought.

Her father had decided one day that the Tooth Fairy was silly and "didn't teach any useful lessons." So he had announced the death of the Tooth Fairy and

39

declared himself Tooth Prince. Now you couldn't just leave your tooth under the pillow and find money in its place in the morning. Instead, you had to *sell* your teeth to the Tooth Prince, and the Tooth Prince drove a very hard bargain. Last time Josie had begun by saying, "You can have this beautiful, shiny tooth for a mere five dollars. It is in mint condition. It has a protective plastic coating applied by a very expensive dentist, and has never had a hole!"

"Five cents," her father said.

"Two fifty," Josie said.

"Five cents," her father said.

"Two dollars even," Josie said. "I mean, look at this gorgeous tooth, Dad. Where can you find another like it?"

"Five cents," her father said.

In the end, he had gotten the tooth for five cents.

This time, though, Josie was going to drive a harder bargain herself. Kim had coached her on when to say, "And that's my final offer," then walk away if he didn't accept it.

"Look at it this way," Kim had said, "what would you do with your teeth if there wasn't any Tooth Fairy . . . or Tooth Prince?"

"Keep them, I guess," Josie said.

"Where?" Kim asked.

"I don't know. In my room, probably."

"Right. Like on your bureau or something, right?"

"Yeah . . ."

"That's the point!" Kim said. "That's just what

they don't want. Parents are afraid that if they don't get the teeth away from the kids, the kids will just keep them lying around."

"Gross," Josie said.

"Yes! Now you're catching on. Do you think parents want teeth lying around all over the house? Maybe even falling on the floor where someone might step on them with bare feet? No way! Parents will do *any*thing to get their kids' teeth from them. It's a seller's market, Josie. Make the Tooth Prince pay top dollar for your teeth. Remember, he wants them more than you do."

So Josie had firmed up her resolve. No more five-cent teeth. And molars were special. If her father wouldn't pay at least a dollar for a molar in good condition, she would keep it—and display it prominently on her bureau.

Josie wiggled her tooth once more and thought of Kim. She smiled. Kim was really a pretty decent sister. Josie would be glad to see her when she got home.

Thirty minutes later Josie punched the doorbell to the upstairs flat and let herself in. Her sleeping bag was under her arm, or part of it was. She hadn't had time to roll it, so it dragged on the stairs behind her as she went up.

Paula Finch met her at the top. She was wearing her reading glasses and clutched a book in one hand. A finger held her place.

"Hi, cutie," Paula said. She reached out and tweaked

Josie on the cheek. Josie hated that, having her cheek tweaked. But she liked it that Paula liked her enough to want to do it.

"I'm going out soon to run some errands," Paula said. "But make yourself at home. Beau should be back any minute."

"Where is he?"

"Out delivering flyers. So he can get some work he says."

"Oh, good." Josie was relieved that the flyers were being distributed without her help.

"I agree," Paula said. "Perhaps if he gets work, it will help keep him out of trouble." She shook her head then and said, "My son . . ." It had a woeful sound.

"Is it all right if I wait in Beau's room?" Josie asked. She attempted to gather the sleeping bag in her arms, so as not to give the impression she would create a mess in his bedroom.

"Certainly," Paula said. "You make yourself comfortable, and I'll see you later on." She put her free arm around Josie's shoulder and gave her a light squeeze.

Josie beamed. She didn't know for sure whether she liked Paula Finch so much because there was something to like about Paula, or whether it was because Paula liked *her* so much. Paula even managed to sound sincere when she called Josie "cutie," though Josie knew she was far too gangly to qualify as cute.

She spread her sleeping bag in the middle of Beau's floor. "This is more like it," she said aloud. It sure beat going around sticking flyers in mail slots. Here she was all alone with Beau's entire collection of comics, *Tin Tin* books, and Gary Larson cartoons.

Josie opened the bottom door of Beau's wall cupboard to rummage. Beau had much more storage space in his room than Josie had in hers, all because Beau's father was clever with wood and had built cupboards along one wall. Of course that meant that Beau's bed had to be under the windows, and that part wasn't so terrific. Josie's parents were careful not to put any beds under windows in case there was an earthquake in the middle of the night. If the glass broke, it could fall on you and cut you to ribbons. That's what her mother always said, "cut you to ribbons." It conjured, for Josie, a picture of people transformed into something you'd cook in a wok.

On the other hand, the experts said a really big earthquake might not arrive for another thirty years. Beau would probably be sleeping someplace else by then—like in his own house, with his own wife and children. If he put his bed under a window, Josie could move it then. She might be around . . . as, say, the wife.

Josie rejected all the Spiderman comics and pulled out two Donald Ducks, a *Tin Tin*, and *Beyond the Far Side*. Then her eye caught an unfamiliar magazine. Was it *Games*? She pulled it out.

Josie sat back abruptly on her heels. The magazine

said *Playboy* right across the front in big, bold letters. She'd heard of it before, on the news. It was the magazine that someone said shouldn't be in 7-Eleven stores because of kids. And now she knew why.

She flipped through it quickly. It was full of pictures of women. Mostly they were naked, or nearly so. And besides that, they didn't seem embarrassed about it! There were even some photos of men. They didn't seem embarrassed either.

Josie felt her cheeks flush hot. She closed the magazine and stuffed it back in the cupboard, at the very bottom of the pile of comics.

Where had Beau gotten it? And did this mean that he had started being interested in girls? Since when? He certainly didn't act especially interested in Josie. She was still just his old friend, more a pal than a girl. Would Beau notice her if she were a naked woman? Did he plan to grow up and marry one?

Josie remembered what it felt like to stand at the side of Rossi Pool in her Speedo bathing suit waiting for her lesson. If Beau planned to marry a naked woman, he would have to move his own furniture.

Josie closed the cupboard, picked up the Gary Larson book, and began looking at the cartoons. It was a little hard to concentrate on them, and sometimes you had to concentrate a lot to get the joke.

She was laughing at one with a caption that read, "The real reason dinosaurs became extinct," when she heard Beau's voice down the hall.

"Josie? You there?"

"Back here, Beau," Josie called.

Beau came in, stepped over Josie, and flopped on his bed. "I'm finished," he said. His clothes were dirty, the pocket was ripped loose from his shirt, and there was a raw-looking scrape across his forehead.

"Good grief, Beau! What happened to you?"

"Guess," Beau said.

"I don't know. I *can't* guess. Oh, no . . . Matt Ventura."

"Bingo."

"Wait right there," Josie said. "I'll get a washcloth." She ran to the bathroom, dipped a washcloth under the cold water, and ran back with it to Beau. "Here," she said, "put this on your head."

"Thanks," Beau said. He covered his face with the cloth and spoke through it. The cloth heaved up and down over his mouth as he spoke. "Some days are luckier than others," he said. "This must have been my lucky day because I found out where Matt Ventura lives."

"Jeez . . ." Josie said. "What did you want to know *that* for?"

"I didn't. I was delivering my flyers when I found it out by accident. I stuck a flyer in this mail slot over on Eighteenth Avenue when all of a sudden the door flies open and there's Ventura yelling, 'What are you doing on my property? This is private property. Get off or I'll break all your bones.'

45

"So I started to explain that I was just delivering these flyers when all of a sudden he exploded out the door and tackled me. I hit the pavement, face first. Then as I stood up, he grabbed my shirt by the pocket and punched me in the stomach. My flyers were blowing down the street in the fog, and he stood there laughing."

"Oh, no," Josie said. For the moment she forgot about Beau's injuries and thought of all those flyers. Her hand began to ache again.

"The worst thing, though, is my mother. She just finished giving me a lecture this morning about getting in any more fights. She kept saying how disappointed in me my father would be because he believes in nonviolence. I tried to explain again about Ventura, but she interrupted me and started talking about Gandhi, this famous pacifist, and said she expected me to resolve my fights in a 'more productive way.' I asked her if this man Gandhi was still alive, and she said no. So then I said probably someone just like Matt Ventura had killed him. That made her really mad, and she started muttering about how it would be ironic if a son of hers became a sociopath. That's graduate school talk for not knowing right from wrong. Then, after she said that, she just looked very sad."

"Well, at least she didn't yell at you," Josie said. Getting yelled at by your parents was one of life's least pleasant experiences. Josie knew because it had happened to her more than once.

"I'd almost rather have her yell than look sad," Beau said. "At least if she yells, she gets over it. But looking sad can go on for days." He lifted the cloth from his face and sat up. Then he fingered the flap of his torn shirt pocket.

"I don't know what I'm going to do about this pocket," he said. "Mom also hates to sew. She's always complaining about how torn up my clothes get. But usually it's something that's easy to explain."

Josie examined the torn pocket. "Do you really need that pocket?" she asked. "Maybe you could just take it the rest of the way off and nobody would notice."

"Good thinking!" Beau said. He got a small pair of scissors from his mother's sewing basket and Josie carefully snipped the stitches that held the rest of the pocket in place. Then she plucked out the tiny threads.

Beau stood back. "How does it look?" he asked.

Josie considered. "Not great," she said finally. The fabric under the pocket was darker than the rest of the shirt. "The pocket's gone, but you can still see where it was. It looks like a pocket shadow now."

Beau sighed. "I think I'll just change my shirt. Maybe she won't see it until she's over being mad or sad, whichever it's going to be."

Beau took his shirt off and rolled it into a ball, then stuffed it into the bottom of his cupboard. He pulled a clean rugby shirt from a drawer and put it on. Josie thought of the magazine.

"Beau . . ." she said.

"Huh?"

"There's a sort of strange magazine in with your comics."

"What magazine?" Beau asked.

Josie thought about how to describe it without saying the name. "It's not about skateboards, and it's not a comic. And it's not . . ."

"Oh, *that* magazine. Yeah, well, that's not actually mine."

"Whose is it then?" Josie asked.

"Technically nobody's, I guess. I found it one night when I was hauling our garbage cans out to the sidewalk for collection day. Someone had left a stack of magazines on top of a can two doors down, so naturally I checked through to see if there was anything good. There was just that one, and a *Sports Illustrated*."

"Huh." Josie stuck her finger in her mouth and wiggled a tooth. She had another question she wanted to ask, and it was making her nervous. She took a deep breath.

"Beau," she said, "do you like those pictures, those women?"

Beau shrugged. "It's not so much that I like them. It's more that they're interesting. Anyhow, I'm going to put it back."

"Oh," Josie said, relieved. Maybe she'd get to explain about windows and earthquakes after all.

Paula Finch arrived home late that afternoon with several bags of groceries, a potted plant, a pair of shoes that had had new heels installed, and a new cover for the ironing board. Josie and Beau helped carry in the groceries and put them away. Then they helped put the new cover on the ironing board.

It was one of Josie's principles that you should be extra helpful any time a parent might be thinking of getting mad at you. That way the explosion might be smaller. It rarely worked.

Paula Finch spent the rest of the afternoon studying, while Josie and Beau stayed out of her way. During dinner she wore a clenched-jaw scowl. Josie discovered that it was hard to eat at a table when one person looked worried and another looked angry and nobody spoke much, even if the food was delicious.

After dinner, when Paula said, "Beau, I'd like to speak with you privately for a few minutes," Josie took her pajamas into the bathroom to change. She spent a long time brushing her teeth.

As she was zipping herself into her sleeping bag, Beau returned. "So what did your mother say?" Josie asked.

"She said she didn't know what she was going to do with me," Beau said. He sounded depressed.

"That's not so bad," Josie said. "I thought she might yell and scream or something. She wasn't nearly as angry as I was thinking she'd be."

"Wrong," Beau said. "It's worse. When my mother says she doesn't know what to do with me, the next thing she usually does is think of something. I get the feeling she's thinking right now."

90/21

Chapter Five

Eager to see Kim, Josie returned downstairs at seven thirty the next morning. At nine o'clock Kim was still asleep. At ten o'clock she was still asleep. At eleven o'clock she was still asleep. It was one thing to have a sister away at camp, but quite another to have her come home and fall asleep for the rest of her life.

Josie sat on the couch and thumped her foot on the under side of the coffee table. "Who ever heard of sleeping until nearly noon?" Josie asked.

"A teenager," her father said. "It goes with the territory." He folded a section of the Sunday paper and chucked it on the floor. Then he unfolded another one.

"Then I've decided not to become a teenager," Josie said. "It's abnormal."

"Somebody talking about me?" a voice asked from the doorway.

"Kim!" Josie jumped up and grabbed her sister in a bear hug. "Welcome back! Today's your day to do the dishes."

"Oh, great," Kim laughed. "Now I'm sure I'm home."

"And guess what else. There's something different about me. See if you can guess."

Kim studied her. "Is it something that shows?"

"Yes."

Kim sat on the couch and cocked her head, first one direction then the other. "I give up," she said. "Unless it's that you're taller, I don't see any difference at all."

"That's it!" Josie said. "I'm not only taller, but now I'm taller than you. Stand up again—I'll show you."

"That's okay," Kim said. "I already knew you were taller than me. You've been taller than me for months. I was only hoping you wouldn't notice until I was about to leave for college."

"You knew?" Josie said. "Why didn't you say anything?"

"Fear of revenge, probably. I don't want you to get any ideas about bossing me around just because you're bigger now."

"Ah, like you used to boss me around, right?" That figured. Kim would hate that.

"Yes. But you needed it, Josie. I don't."

"That's all you know," Josie said. It was her opinion that she could have survived quite nicely without Kim's bossing. After all, that was what parents were for, and they usually did plenty. Maybe revenge wasn't such a bad idea. "I don't think I want to boss you," Josie said.

"That's a relief."

"I'll take your room instead."

"My room?!" Kim screeched.

"Sure," Josie said. "After all, I take up more space in the world than you do now. So I should have the bigger room. That's reasonable, isn't it?"

"No! It sounds very *un*reasonable if you ask me. Dad, tell her—she can't have my room, can she?"

Their father lowered his paper and looked over it. "You can't have Kim's room," he said. "Room assignments are based on seniority, not size." He put the paper back up.

"Whew!" Kim said.

Josie groaned and slumped back on the couch. There wasn't any justice. After twelve years as the smallest one in the family, being taller than Kim should have some advantages. But so far Josie couldn't think of one.

She stuck a finger in her mouth and gave one of her loose molars a hard shove. Suddenly her finger was in a hole and the tooth was in her lap.

"Would you look at that!" she said, holding it up. "My tooth came out."

"Hey!" her father said. "That's great. Would you like to sell it now? I'll give you five cents. Unless it has a hole, of course. I can't pay as much for a tooth with cavities." He tossed aside another section of the paper.

"Never mind," Josie said, shoving the tooth into

her jeans pocket. "I'll sell it to you later. When I feel stronger."

Sandy Pucinski came into the living room with a cup of coffee. "So what are you going to do with your day?" she asked Kim. "Or what's left of it, now that you've caught up with your beauty sleep?"

"Dishes, probably," Kim laughed. "But after that I think I'll unpack, then write to some of my friends from camp."

"But you just left them yesterday," her mother said.

"Well, I may just write to Keith," Kim said. She began to pick at something invisible on her arm.

"Who's Keith?" Josie asked.

"A bassoonist," her father said. "With muscles." He opened another section of the paper and gave it a snap. It wasn't the same as saying *humph*, but it had a similar tone.

Josie looked from Kim to her father and back. "Is Keith your boyfriend?" she asked.

"Sort of," Kim said. "Well, no, not exactly. It's more like we're just good friends. I danced with him a lot at the dances is all, and we were in a trio to-gether."

"That's what you said about what's-his-name—the violinist you fell madly in love with last year," Sandy Pucinski said.

"Mom . . ." Kim sounded exasperated.

Their father must have found something funny in the paper because he started to chuckle.

"Dad . . ." Kim began. Then she gave up. "You're all impossible," she said. "I should never open my mouth around here."

"But Kim," her mother said, "it's perfectly normal and healthy to have a boyfriend at your age."

Kim groaned.

"It's just that I thought you said he lived in Stockton. Isn't that a little far away?"

"That's what letters are for," Kim said. "And cars. Keith drives a car. He said he might be able to come to San Francisco some weekend."

"Uh-huh," Bill Pucinski said. "Now let me get this straight: he'll need a place to stay, so you'll want to offer him our sofa bed. And while he's here, you will spend every minute with him and maybe go out to a movie or two. But he's not your boyfriend, right?"

"*Dad* . . ." Kim said.

It sounded terribly romantic to Josie. And slightly unbelievable. Most of her friends thought that kids who played in orchestras were nerds. But Josie was beginning to suspect that Kim had stumbled onto a terrific deal. Kim hadn't been without a boyfriend for more than a week in three years—and all of them played instruments, and all of them were cute.

If she wasn't going to be a total dud as a teenager, Josie thought maybe she should give music another chance. Of course Kim had played cello for years and years. Josie wondered if it was too late.

"If I started playing an instrument now," she asked,

"would I be good enough to go to music camp by the time I'm sixteen? I was thinking I could try flute again. Either that or drums."

"Oh, Josie," her mother said, "wanting to go to music camp isn't a good enough reason to take up an instrument. Anyhow, you're not musical. Or rather, you don't like music much."

"Both," Josie said. "But it doesn't seem fair that Kim gets to go away to camp every year just because she's talented, and I have to stay home because I'm not. Don't they have camps for kids with no talents?"

"You're not untalented," her father said. "We just haven't discovered yours yet. It's probably the slow-acting kind."

"Well, do they have a special camp for kids who are going to discover their talents later?" Josie asked.

"I don't know," her mother said. "Besides, camps are expensive. We send Kim because she needs it; it helps her development as a musician."

"Well, *my* development could use some help," Josie said. "All I get for hanging around the city all summer is gummy hair from the chlorine in Rossi Pool—and a talent for dodging drug pushers."

"Drug pushers!" both her parents said in unison.

"Good for you," Kim said. "You just spoke the magic word. I think you just won yourself a whole summer away at camp, Josie."

"Josie," Sandy Pucinski said, "has someone really tried to sell you drugs?"

Josie hesitated. She'd never mentioned the drug pushers to her parents because she was afraid they'd lock her in the house all summer for safety. Besides, she would never take drugs, so what was the big deal? On the other hand, if her parents wanted to send her to camp for the entire summer just to protect her . . .

"Well," Josie said, "actually somebody tried to give me some for free. This older kid came up to me and Beau at Aragon Playground and offered us these red and black pills. But we said no thanks, and he left when the playground supervisor came out of the building."

"Good Lord," her mother said.

"Then another time I saw some guys selling something to these little kids near the concourse in Golden Gate Park. But Beau and I just stayed away."

"Good girl," her father said. "I'm really proud of you."

Even though she knew her father meant to pay her a compliment, Josie felt faintly insulted. "Maybe I'm not talented, but I'm not stupid, Dad. Good grief. What would I want drugs for? I don't even like to take the medicine the doctor gives me."

"Well, I'm relieved to hear it," her father said.

"I don't know, Bill . . ." Sandy Pucinski looked worried. "Maybe the city isn't the right place for children to spend the summer. Why expose them to unnecessary risks?" It was the same thing she said when the dentist wanted to take X rays.

"Oh, swell," Kim said. "Then I think you'd better start planning to buy a house in the suburbs, because there are kids selling drugs in all the schools here, too. I think a house with a pool would be nice."

Bill Pucinski cleared his throat. "There are drug problems in the suburbs, too. The papers are full of it. It *might* be safe out in the country, but Antarctica would be even better. No, I think we need to rely on our girls to have good sense." He was using his This-Is-Official voice.

Josie sagged. For a minute there she had almost been able to smell the Ponderosa pine at her future camp in the Sierra. But then Kim had to open her big mouth and spoil it. She made a face at her sister.

"Of course," Kim said, "you *could* send Josie to camp just because she wants to go. And if you sent her at the same time you sent me, you could have a vacation without us. A lot of my friends' parents go away while their kids are at camp."

"Hey!" Bill Pucinski said.

"Hmmmm," Sandy Pucinski said.

Josie looked at Kim and grinned.

She spent the early afternoon helping Kim unpack. And she didn't object when Kim asked her to carry the dirty clothes to the laundry room. Even dirty, Kim's clothes didn't seem so bad now that Josie knew she'd never have to wear them. And unpacking was educational; Josie would need to know what to take when she went to camp herself next summer.

When Kim shooed Josie from her room so she could write to Keith, Josie went to her own room and began another list.

What To Pack For Camp
1. Hair curlers
2. Mouthwash
3. Small mirror
4. Clearasil

Beau arrived at three to ask if Josie would like to come with him to meet his first customer. Josie's list wasn't complete, but she had a full year to work on it, so she figured there was no rush.

"This is actually my second customer," Beau said as they biked down Cabrillo Street. "The first was a lady who wondered if I was experienced in baby-sitting for infants. I told her 'not much.' But then she asked me if I knew how to change diapers, and since I didn't want to sound *too* dumb, I said yes. Next she asked me to come over to demonstrate, and all the way there I worried about whether I would stick the baby with a pin."

"Nobody uses pins any more," Josie said. "All you have to do is stick the adhesive tab to the diaper. You can't miss."

"That's what I found out. Only I did miss. I stuck the adhesive to the baby, and when I pulled it off, the baby cried. I don't think she's going to call me to baby-sit."

Beau's second customer turned out to be an elderly lady who was recovering from a broken hip. She had an old and very overweight Chihuahua that needed to be carried down the back steps twice a day so it could "do its duty" in the yard. The lady said her doctor had told her it would be another month before she could carry Conchita down the steps herself. She offered Beau twenty-five cents a trip to do it for her.

While Beau was inside Mrs. Sloane's house carrying the Chihuahua back and forth, Josie stayed with their bikes and added it up. Twenty-five cents twice a day for thirty days came out to fifteen dollars for the month.

When Beau returned, Josie said, "All you need is three jobs like Mrs. Sloane's, and you'll have a skateboard you can ride by the end of the summer."

Josie and Beau rode their bikes into Golden Gate Park from the Rose Garden entrance on Fulton Street. The park was closed to automobile traffic on Sundays, and you could ride your bike or roller-skate right down JFK Drive.

Josie liked to race, even though she had never yet won a race with Beau. She kept thinking that someday she might win, especially now that she was bigger than he was. She hoped he wouldn't mind too much.

At full speed they wound their way through the crowds of people on JFK Drive, bounced across a meadow, and then puffed up a hill until they got to Stow Lake.

"I'll need more jobs than that if I get into any more fights with Matt Ventura," Beau said. They had stopped to catch their breath by the lake. "My mother says that the next time I get into a fight with him she's going to 'withdraw her offer of financial support.' Roughly translated, that means she won't pay for the helmet and pads I need to go with my skateboard, and since she says I'm not allowed to ride a skateboard without them, I really need her help."

"But that's not fair," Josie said.

"She thinks it is," Beau said. "This morning she told me all about how she and my dad had gone on peace marches and sit-ins when they were in college, and she said they didn't expect to raise a child who 'settled his conflicts through violence.' Then she said again how disappointed my dad would be in me if he knew about my behavior. The way she said it, I had the feeling he's going to hear about it very soon."

"Oh no," Josie said. She knew Beau would hate having his father disappointed in him. "She can't mean all that, Beau."

"She means it," Beau said.

"But you're not even fighting. It's like you're the fight*ee*, not the fight*er*."

"Try telling that to my mother," Beau said. "Anyway, I've got a plan partly worked out. See, I figure the smartest thing to do is just avoid Ventura; then I can't get into any trouble. So I've decided to quit swimming for starters. I'll use swim time to carry out

Mrs. Sloane's dog and do any other jobs that come along. That way while Ventura is safely splashing around Rossi Pool, I can be out making money."

"That means I'll have to go to swimming lessons alone," Josie said, "all for the privilege of getting worse by the day and listening to Don yell 'Laps!' Maybe I should quit, too." Then she thought. "No, I can't. I might get to go to camp next summer, and they probably expect you to know how to swim."

"I'd like to go to camp," Beau said. "Today. But then I still wouldn't make any money, so I'd never get my skateboard."

Josie watched as a woman tossed popcorn into the lake for the ducks. The big ducks always seemed to shove the smaller ones out of the way. They didn't share.

Sometimes Josie used to imagine that it would be nice to have Paula Finch for a mother instead of her own. But Josie knew she wouldn't want her now— not if Paula was going to make up punishments that didn't fit crimes that hadn't even been committed. Josie would stick with her own parents, flawed as they were.

"Well, okay then," Josie said. "Avoiding Matt Ventura probably is the smartest thing to do, at least until you've got your skateboard. Or until he moves to Texas, which would be even better. But from now on, if we even *see* Ventura, we just run like mad the other direction. It's the only way."

"I guess so," Beau said gloomily. "But I'll tell you, Josie, I think I'd rather get my skateboard *and* punch Ventura's lights out, too. I don't know why I should be a pacifist just because my parents are. They're not the ones who are getting beat up."

Josie was suddenly sorry she wasn't the kind to save money. Once she had added it up: if she'd saved all of her money since she had first begun getting an allowance, she'd have more than three hundred dollars —more than enough to help Beau buy his skateboard.

"If I had some money, I'd give it to you," Josie said.

"No . . . that's okay."

"But I don't. Right now I don't even have any prospects," she said. "Unless you count teeth." She thought for a minute. "I wonder if ten dollars is too much to ask for a molar."

Chapter Six

Josie was late for her swimming lesson on Monday, even though she had taken the bus. When she got to the pool, Don yelled at her, "Hey, you!"

"Me?" Josie asked.

"Yes, you! Fifteen kicks, fifteen rhythmic breathings, and then laps. And don't be late again. I don't like it."

Josie shook her head. She spent most of the swimming lesson walking back and forth across the pool, trying to figure out by what mistake Don had become a swim instructor. Like maybe he had been hired to clean the pool but had misunderstood.

Once Josie looked over to where Matt Ventura was swimming laps. He was a pretty strong swimmer. Josie wasn't sure he even needed to take lessons, unless he wanted to swim competitively. He had large muscles for a kid, Josie noticed. Even the tattooed snake looked muscular.

On Tuesday Josie arrived on time for swimming,

but Don was absent. Josie wondered whether he was sick or had just gotten lost. If he was sick, he might take a long time to recover.

Cathy took over Don's class. The first thing she did was ask everyone to do the back float. Most of the kinds from Don's class sank. Josie hadn't done the back float in so long that she went straight down and came up spluttering.

"Keep your head back, Josie!" Cathy yelled.

"Oh, yeah," Josie said. "I forgot." She put her head back and floated. She was glad Cathy had remembered her name.

When it came time to do the crawl stroke, Josie took off, chugging hard. In a few seconds everyone was ahead of her as usual. Cathy called her to the side of the pool.

"What are you doing, Josie?"

"I'm *trying*," Josie protested. She hadn't even gotten to the part where she walked yet.

"But your arms. What are you doing with your arms? You look like a windmill."

"I'm trying to keep my arms as straight as possible when they go over my head," Josie said. "But it's hard."

"No wonder you're having trouble," Cathy said. "The point isn't what you do with your arms when they're *out* of the water so much as what you do with them when they're *in* the water." She ducked her head and stuck her arms out in front to demonstrate.

"It's like this," she said. "Pull. Pull. You try to pull yourself through the water, and to do that you have to move the water with your arms. Think of yourself as moving water."

"Okay," Josie said.

"And when you kick, the idea is to make the smallest splash possible, not the biggest. Keep your legs straight."

"Okay," Josie said. She had been priding herself on her big splash.

"And Josie? Don't try so hard, all right? You make it look like such hard work. Swimming is really fun once you get the hang of it." Cathy smiled at Josie.

Josie pushed off from the side of the pool and imagined herself moving water, slowly but powerfully. And she kept her legs straight, even though it felt as though she wasn't doing as much work as she should. In a few minutes she had doubled her speed. By the end of class she was swimming as fast as everyone else. She was so happy that when she went to the locker room she forgot to huddle her arms across her chest as she walked.

On Wednesday Don returned. But by then Josie had worked out a plan for herself. She positioned herself as close as she could to Cathy's class, and when Don told everyone to start swimming laps, Josie did the back float with the kids in Cathy's class. Don never noticed.

When Cathy started giving kids pointers on the

65

backstroke, Josie listened until she thought she had heard enough. Then she started swimming the backstroke across the pool. You didn't need rhythmic breathing to do the backstroke.

As Josie left Rossi Pool, she spotted Matt Ventura leaning on a pole. "Hey," he said as Josie walked past him, "where's your friend?"

"What friend?" Josie asked, as if she didn't know.

"Pretty Bird," Matt said. "That is his name, isn't it? Pretty Bird?"

"I don't know what you're talking about," Josie said. She started to walk on.

"Beau Finch. That's what 'Beau' means—pretty. And a finch is a kind of bird. So I figure his name is Pretty Bird. It's a sissy name, just like your friend."

Josie started to say that "Beau" happened to be short for Beaumont, which was a family name on Beau's mother's side and didn't have anything to do with Beau's looks so far as Josie knew. But somehow Josie sensed that Matt wouldn't be too interested in the origins of Beau's name. She kept walking.

At the top of the steps Matt suddenly jumped in front of her and blocked her way. "So where is he, huh? I figure you know, so I'm asking . . . nice."

Josie's mind began to race. She should say something. Anything. Make something up. "He's away," she said.

"Oh yeah? Where?"

"At . . . uh . . . camp. Somebody offered him a chance to go to camp, a scholarship, so he went. In fact, he's going to be away for the rest of the summer. It's a real neat camp, see." She added that last part to make it sound more realistic.

"Oh, sure," Matt said. "And I just won a free trip to Disneyland. Tell Pretty Bird I'm looking for him, you hear? And when I find him"—Matt slammed his fist into his palm—"he's dead meat." He turned and left Josie standing at the top of the steps.

Josie watched him as he walked away. He had a walk that she had seen in the movies—swaggering, but with his arms tensed and his fists balled up. He looked like he was ready for a fight every second. Her heart was pounding just from talking with him.

At home Josie dumped her wet bathing suit in the utility room and went upstairs. Beau was at his desk, a back issue of *Thrasher* magazine open in front of him.

"I'm glad you're here," Beau said. "Come look at this. I've worked it all out. First there's the deck, of course—that's already picked out. But then there are the trucks. I've decided now—it's definite—I'm getting Independent trucks. And then look here." He flipped the page to where he had circled several items in red. "I'll get a Powell/Perralta nose guard. Some color that will look cool with black, since the deck is black. Then I want NMB bearings for the wheels. The bearings are extra, of course. . . ."

"Beau . . ." Josie said. She didn't want to hear all this.

"Just a minute," he said. "Then I'll get a Tracker

lapper. You need that to protect the trucks going over curbs. And I'll get this tail skid here." He pointed. "And these rails that match the nose guard. The only thing I haven't absolutely decided on yet is the wheels, but right now I'm leaning toward the Kryptonic Super Ultralite, though they cost a bit more."

"*Beau*," Josie said.

"Oh yeah—the helmet and pads, too. I wish I could just skip them, but Mom says no way. Anyhow, a black helmet might be sort of cool, and Rector makes these sharp elbow pads. So . . . what do you think, Josie?"

Josie sighed. "I think you're going to be very happy," she said.

"Yeah." Beau beamed. "This magazine has the exact prices on everything, so I know just how much longer I'll have to carry Conchita around for Mrs. Sloane. That dog is so stupid I don't think it knows *how* to walk."

"Beau," Josie said, "does your mother know you don't go to swimming lessons anymore?"

Beau closed the magazine and put it in the cupboard. It flashed through Josie's mind that if Beau had to be so crazy about a magazine, she was just as glad it was *Thrasher* instead of a certain other one.

"I don't know," Beau said.

"What do you mean you don't know?"

"She asked me this morning how swimming was going, so I told her I wasn't making much progress.

68

Which is really the truth. But I don't know whether she knows *why* I'm not making much progress."

"I am," Josie said. "Making progress, that is."

"Whoa!" Beau said. "What happened, did Don get a brain transplant or something?"

"No, I worked out another system. But the main thing is that I'm improving. At last."

"So maybe when you go to camp next summer, you won't drown in the South Fork of the Toulomne River?"

"Yeah . . ." It gave Josie a small pang to realize that if she went away to camp next year she would be apart from Beau. Still, she reasoned, it would most likely only be for a week or two. And Beau would think she was dumb if she said she might miss him.

"What are you going to say if your mother figures out you've quit swimming?" Josie asked. If Matt Ventura started to harass her or if she couldn't continue her lessons with Cathy, Josie might want to quit, too. It would help to know what to tell her parents.

"I don't know," Beau said. "But I'm not going to worry about it. For all I know, she won't even care. You don't need swimming lessons to be a skateboarding champion, after all."

Beau picked up a large ball bearing and plunked it down the chute of the model roller coaster he had sitting on his desk. It whizzed down a hill, went around two curves, then flew off.

69

"Needs adjustment," he said.

"Beau, let's go ice-skating today, okay? I'll pay."

"I don't know," Beau said.

"Come on," Josie said. "It would be fun. And if you're worried about my money, don't be. I got my allowance today, and it's nearly free anyhow because we can go with the Aragon Playground group. All we have to pay for is skates."

"You mean on one of those playground field trips?" Beau asked. "No way. Ventura usually goes on those —at least the good ones. With my luck, he'd be sure to be there. And he'd do something noticeable like trip me on the ice, then skate on my face. No thanks."

Josie wanted to protest, but she knew Beau was right. Matt usually did show up at the activities that were fun and cheap, like the trip to Marine World.

Josie went to Beau's window and looked out. The fog was higher today and lighter, and off in the distance she could see a strip of blue sky. It would probably be sunny if they just went far enough east, like to the playground in Golden Gate Park.

"Matt's looking for you anyhow," she admitted.

"He is? I mean, I'm sure he is—but how do you know?"

"He told me," Josie said. "But I told him you had gone away to camp for the rest of the summer."

"Good thinking, Josie!"

"It would have been, but I don't think he bought it." Josie played with the ring on the window shade. "Still, maybe we could go someplace that *isn't* the ice-skating rink, Beau. It would probably be safe, because you're right that Matt will most likely go ice-skating with the field trip kids."

"Well . . ." Beau joined Josie at the window and peered out. "Maybe," he said. Josie's hopes rose. "Naw . . . any risk, even a small one, is too big. I mean when you think of my whole career on a skateboard versus an afternoon fooling around outside, it's just not worth it. I think I'll pass, Josie. Sorry."

Josie groaned. "What are we going to *do*, Beau? Are we going to spend the rest of the summer at home because of Matt Ventura and a skateboard?"

"No," Beau said. "I have my jobs. And you can go anyplace you like. By the way, I got another job today. I'm going to wash and wax this guy's car on Saturday."

"Swell," Josie said. "In other words, except for your jobs you're not going outside for the rest of the summer, and we can't go anyplace together."

"Well . . ." Beau looked thoughtful. Then he said, "Tell you what, Josie. We can do any *in*side thing you want. Like if you want to play Trivial Pursuit all afternoon, that's okay with me. So long as it's indoors, I'll agree to it."

"I think I'll go home," Josie said. She headed toward the door.

"Josie . . ."

"I'll come back when I've thought of something I'd like to do. *In*doors."

"Josie . . ."

"Like play dolls," Josie said. She walked out.

"*Josie!*"

Josie slammed the front door of her flat when she went in. It would serve Beau right if she did make him play dolls. He'd hate that worse than anything. He'd always refused when they were younger, but now here he was saying he'd do *any*thing so long as it was indoors. Playing dolls was almost too good for him.

The trouble was that Josie was about three years past playing dolls herself. Even Barbie and Ken seemed pretty lame now. But in a strange way, nothing had arrived to take its place. She liked books well enough, but there wasn't anything to play that she enjoyed as much as she once enjoyed dolls or dressing up or even building forts with Beau. She felt stuck at an in-between place—in between being sophisticated and grown-up like Kim's friends, and being a kid.

She heard the sounds of Kim's cello through her bedroom door—something slow and moody-sounding, the same few notes over and over. Josie went to the door and knocked.

"Come in," Kim called.

Josie walked to Kim's bed and stretched out on it. She rested her cheek on Kim's bear.

"What would you do," Josie asked, "if you had this best friend who happened to be a boy and all of a sudden he started to get really weird?"

"Hmmm . . ." Kim said.

"Well, it's not sudden, exactly. He's been getting weird for a while. But it's suddenly gotten worse."

Kim grinned. "I presume you mean Beau," she said. "And if I were you, I'd tell him you're not ready to hold hands until you're sure it's real love. That usually does it."

"It's not *that*," Josie said. "The only thing Beau's in love with these days is a skateboard."

"That's good. He's a little young to go steady anyhow, if you ask me." Kim balanced her bow on one finger and watched it totter.

"Come on," Josie said. "This is serious. Beau's turning into a hermit. He won't go anyplace anymore, all because of a skateboard."

"That's pretty weird all right," Kim said.

"So what should I do? What would *you* do, Kim? You're the big sister—you're supposed to give me advice."

"Well," she said, "if I were you, I'd do nothing and wait. In a few years Beau will trade in his skateboard for a car, and then you can start going places together again. That's my advice, free of charge." She turned back to her music stand and played something very intricate and fast on only two strings.

"You're a big help," Josie said. She shoved the bear away, walked over to Kim's music stand, and closed the piece of music Kim was looking at. "My advice to you is to do nothing for a few years and see if Juilliard sends you an engraved invitation," she said.

"Thanks a lot," Kim said.

"No charge."

Chapter Seven

After her swimming lesson on Thursday, Josie telephoned three girls from her class at Presidio Middle School. One of them wasn't home and the other two were busy. It occurred to Josie that perhaps it wasn't such a great idea to have only one best friend because if that best friend moved away or pooped out, you could end up with nobody.

She took Trivial Pursuit upstairs and played with Beau all afternoon.

"Does hiding out include not going to the fireworks at Crissy Field tomorrow?" Josie asked. "Kim said she'd take us again this year." Until a few years ago the Finches and the Pucinskis had always had a combined family picnic at Crissy Field on the Fourth of July. But as soon as Kim had gotten old enough to go on her own, the adults confessed that they didn't really enjoy the mobs of people, the traffic jams, or sitting on the hard ground in the cold night air, so they had put Kim in charge of the expedition.

"It's not called hiding out. It's called being careful. And of course I'm going to Crissy Field. Why not?"

"Because Matt Ventura might be there, that's why not."

"Yes, but so will half of San Francisco," Beau said. "He'd never find me in the crowd."

Josie wasn't so sure. It was true that thousands and thousands of people turned out to watch the fireworks, but inevitably Josie would see a few people she knew from school. And last year Kim ran into her boyfriend there with another girl. "I didn't know you'd be here," he had said to Kim. Kim thought it over and decided that wasn't a good enough excuse, so she broke up with him anyway.

"Besides," Beau said. "I've never missed a Fourth of July at Crissy Field yet. My mother says she took me even before I was born, inside her."

At two o'clock the next afternoon, Josie, Beau, Kim, and Kim's friend Valerie got on the No. 28 to Crissy Field. The bus was jammed with people all on their way to the same place, and Beau slipped on unnoticed with a transfer that wasn't even the right color.

The four of them took turns carrying the blanket and the small cooler that the Pucinskis had packed with pita-bread sandwiches, deviled eggs, cookies, and soft drinks. It was the same picnic they took every year.

Kim and Valerie were picky about where to spread their blanket, and spent a long time choosing. They walked back and forth looking at empty spaces, say-ing, "What do you think?" to each another, elimi-nating all the places that were near crying babies (too noisy) or couples making out (too embarrassing). Sometimes they would head back to a spot that had maybe been all right after all, only to find someone else had taken it. Josie decided that what they were really looking for was a space next to a couple of cute boys their own age.

They ended up wedged between an old couple in folding chairs, a family with a happy-looking baby, and a group of about fifteen teenagers, all of whom seemed to be talking at once.

"We either have to stay with our food or carry it with us," Kim said. "I think we should take turns staying with the blanket. So who wants to go first?"

Josie rolled her eyes. Every year they took turns staying with the blanket, but here was Kim acting like it was some brand-new idea she'd just invented. That was one of Kim's few faults: when she was with a friend her own age, she often began treating Josie as though she were a third-grader, barely capable of thinking for herself.

Josie saw Beau eyeing the cooler. "We'll stay," she said.

"Suit yourself," Kim said, "but remember you can't leave until we get back."

"Yes, sir!" Josie saluted.

Kim smiled. She seemed to take it as a compliment. She and Valerie disappeared into the crowd. Josie and Beau dug into the pita-bread sandwiches and watched the passing show. People of every race came by carrying coolers and blankets, small groups of people passed, looking as though they were on their way to costume parties, and Yuppies glided by, pushing babies in Aprica strollers.

In the distance Josie could hear the sounds of a rock band. She was glad Kim and Valerie had gone off first because the rock band would be done by the time they returned. Josie preferred the Dixieland band that usually played later, or even the bluegrass band with the mandolin.

Kim and Valerie were gone a long time. Josie and Beau were beginning to wonder if they'd gotten lost by the time they returned, each carrying a cone of half-eaten cotton candy.

"Wow! Where did you get that?" Beau asked.

"Way down at the other end of the field," Valerie said. "But I think you should hurry if you want some. They were running out when we got these."

Josie and Beau scrambled to their feet and took off running to the other end of Crissy Field. The man who ran the cotton candy machine was packing up as they arrived.

"Rats," Josie said.

Beau laughed. "It doesn't matter because I didn't have any money anyway."

"I did," Josie said. She held her stomach. "Maybe it's just as well. I'm so stuffed I've got a stitch in my side from running."

They found their way to the stage where a jazz band had just finished playing and the Dixieland band was setting up. Josie and Beau waited, and when the band began to play "When the Saints Come Marching In," the crowd let out a cheer. Josie and Beau stayed until the end of the set, clapping and stomping their feet with the rest of the crowd.

Next they went to watch a woman who was doing face painting. Most of her customers were little kids, and Josie knew why. Her father had let her have her face painted once years ago, and when the afternoon sun got hot it had smeared. Later the colors ran onto the ice cream Josie was eating. And by sunset her whole face itched. Face painting was an activity you only needed to do once.

Josie and Beau wandered farther up Crissy Field to where a crowd had gathered around a pair of jugglers. They were really good. Josie decided they must have been imported from Ghirardelli Square. All of the best jugglers worked Ghirardelli Square or Pier 39 because that was where the rich tourists shopped.

One of the jugglers was working with knives. He juggled them high over his head and caught them behind his back.

"Those knives are fake," Josie said.

"They're not," Beau said. "My father told me they're real knives."

"Then they're just dull, that's all."

"No, they're not. They're sharp. I saw one guy slice a melon with one. They could chop your head off."

"So how come the jugglers don't get all sliced up?" Josie asked.

"I don't know," Beau said. "I guess they're just very, very good jugglers. That's why they make so much money." He sounded wistful. A hat on the ground in front of the jugglers was overflowing with donations, most of it in bills, some as large as twenty dollars. It looked like a fortune, and you could see that Beau was wondering how good he would have to get at juggling to buy his skateboard.

In a minute the jugglers were tossing the knives back and forth between them. Once the first stepped back and let the knife fall to the wooden platform. The knife embedded itself, tip down, and vibrated back and forth. People in the crowd sucked in their breaths.

Suddenly Josie gripped Beau by the upper arm. "Look," she whispered, pointing across the crowd.

"Uh-oh," Beau said. Standing not thirty feet away from them, in plain view, with his fists jammed in his pockets and staring straight up at the jugglers, was Matt Ventura.

"Let's get out of here before he spots us," Beau said.

They began to push their way through to the outer edges of the crowd, Beau in front, hauling Josie by the wrist.

"Hurry," Beau said.

Josie glanced back over her shoulder. Matt Ventura was looking straight at her. He pulled his hands from his pockets, whirled, and began to shove his way out through the crowd behind him.

"He saw us!" Josie said. "Run! We have to run!"

Breaking out of the crowd, Josie and Beau began to sprint, dodging and weaving around blankets and people who were picnicking or milling about. Josie didn't look where she was going. She just focused on Beau's back and followed him as he ducked through the throng.

Finally, Beau pulled up short near a crowd of people who were gathered around a souvenir vendor, a man selling pennants, caps, and small replicas of the Statue of Liberty.

Beau looked around. "I think we lost him," he said. He was panting.

"I hope so," Josie said, clutching her side. "Can you get a ruptured appendix from running?"

"I don't think so. But come on, let's find the blanket. We can't be far away, and I think we should lie low for a while just in case."

Josie followed Beau as before. Then, as she looked back over her shoulder to see if they were being followed, she ran smack into Beau from behind. He had stopped.

"What . . ." Josie said. Then she saw.

Right in front of Beau, not four feet away, stood

Matt Ventura. He was pushing the sleeves up on his arms.

"Got you, you wimp," he said. "You Pretty Bird coward."

"Run," Josie yelled. She yanked Beau by the arm.

But Beau stood his ground. He wrenched his arm free from Josie and doubled up his fists. Too late. Matt Ventura was on him, and suddenly they were both on the ground, Ventura on top, pounding Beau in the side. Beau was swinging with his fists too, but he couldn't get out from under Matt's weight, and his swings lacked force.

Just as Josie had decided to leap on Matt's back and bite him or pull his hair, he landed a hard right to Beau's cheekbone, then jumped up and ran away.

Josie reached down to help Beau to his feet, but he shook her off. "Leave me alone," he said. "I should have jumped him first, then he'd have something to run for." He staggered to his feet.

"Good thing you didn't," Josie said. "Then you'd have really been in trouble."

"Trouble!" Beau was indignant. "If my face looks like it feels, I'm already going to be in as much trouble as I could possibly be in. And I didn't even have the satisfaction of breaking that sucker's nose."

"But Beau . . ." Josie said. That was pretty strong talk coming from Beau. Well, he had a right to be upset. She reached out and tried to brush some of the loose grass from his shirt.

"Women!" Beau said. He turned and stalked off in the direction of the blanket.

Josie stood there feeling stunned. What had she done wrong? It seemed that Beau was mad at *her*. She'd only tried to help. He was supposed to be mad at Matt Ventura, not Josie. And what had he meant by "women"? Was this attitude something that happened to boys when they were about to become teenagers—did they become chauvinists?

It was weird, but Josie had the feeling she understood Beau less and less with every passing day.

Slowly, Josie found her way back to the blanket. Beau was already there, lying down, holding an unopened can of Orange Crush to his left eye.

Josie sank to her knees. "Where are Kim and Valerie?" she asked.

"I told them they could go," Beau said. "And I told them to stay as long as they liked. I've seen everything I want to see, and more."

Josie just stared at Beau, feeling bleak. Then she realized that what she wanted was a cookie. Not just wanted, needed. She opened the cooler and found the pack of cookies. Most of them were gone. Valerie and Kim must have been very hungry.

The cookies had chocolate icing. Josie began to lick it off one, slowly. "I think you're supposed to put a steak on that eye," she said at last.

"No, that's just in cartoons. The steak is because it's cold, but this soft drink is plenty cold."

"Can I see?" Josie asked.

Beau lifted up the can of Crush. His cheek and eye were all red and slightly glistening with moisture from the cold can. His eye was swollen and only about half open.

"How does it look?" he asked.

"Not too good, Beau."

Beau moaned.

"But keep the cold can on it," she said. "Maybe it will be less puffy by the time we get home."

Beau probed around his cheek and eye with his fingers. Then he put the can back on his face. "I think it's a waste of effort," he said. "But I guess I have nothing to lose."

By the time Kim and Valerie returned, it was nearly dark. Josie watched the fireworks without much enthusiasm. She didn't know whether it was Beau's predicament that was depressing her or the fact that the fog had rolled in and it was cold. In any case, it was hard to get enthusiastic about fireworks that went up just a short way and then got swallowed by a ceiling of fog.

Kim and Valerie had struck up a conversation with the teenagers next to them and had all but moved to their blanket. They seemed oblivious to Josie's and Beau's subdued states. Josie was glad when it was time to go home.

As they walked up the front steps of their building, Josie whispered to Beau, "If it's like last year, I'll bet your mother is in our flat with my parents. So maybe you can sneak in and go straight to bed."

"So I can get yelled at in the morning instead of tonight?" Beau asked.

"No," Josie said. "So maybe by morning your face will look normal and nobody will ever know."

"Fat chance," Beau said. "But anything's worth a try."

The door to the flat clicked shut quietly behind Beau. "Good luck," Josie murmured.

Just as Josie had predicted, Paula Finch was sitting in the living room with her parents. They were laughing about something in voices that Josie thought were too loud, and she had to stand there for a minute to get their attention.

Then Sandy Pucinski said, "Oh, Josie, how were the fireworks?"

"They were fine," Josie said.

"I'm glad," her mother said. She turned back to say something to Paula.

"Dad," Josie said, "could I see you in the kitchen for a minute? Alone?"

Her father looked momentarily surprised, then said, "Sure, kiddo," and followed Josie into the kitchen. "What is it?" he asked.

"It's about the tooth," Josie said. "I want to sell it."

"Now?" her father asked.

"Yes, now. It's really important, because I'm going to need the money for something special."

Her father shrugged. "Okay," he said. "I'll offer you five cents."

"That's the thing, Dad. Five cents isn't much for a tooth, you'll have to admit."

"Granted . . ."

"And this is a molar. Plus, it is in el-primo mint condition and has had only one previous owner."

"Okay, okay," he father said. "Ten cents."

"Ten dollars," Josie said.

"Ten dollars!" her father practically yelled.

"I told you it's important, Dad. I really need the money. It's for a good cause, believe me."

"Twenty-five cents," he said.

"Ten dollars," Josie said. She took a deep breath. "And that's my final offer."

"Keep the tooth," Bill Pucinski said. He turned and left the room.

Chapter Eight

Josie was fidgety the next morning. She wanted to rush upstairs and see what had happened to Beau's eye. But on the other hand, if Paula Finch was doing any hollering, Josie preferred to stay out of the way.

She made herself French toast for breakfast, and then, about an hour later when Kim finally got up, Josie made some for her, too. She did the dishes because it was her turn, and even dried them and put them away, just for something to do.

Later Josie rummaged around in her mother's sewing chest and found a scrap of fabric that suited her. It was a small piece of black velvet, a scrap left over from a skirt her mother had made for Kim to wear at orchestra performances. Josie cut the scrap into the shape of a star. Then she laid it carefully on her dresser top. Right in the center she set her tooth.

By noon it seemed to Josie that even a furious mother would be finished hollering, so she pushed the doorbell to the Finch flat and let herself in.

Paula Finch met her at the top of the stairs. She was wearing her reading glasses and holding a book. The title on the book said, *Your Pre-Adolescent: The Difficult Years.* Josie had the idea Paula was studying up on Beau.

"Beau is down in the garage," Paula Finch said. "He tells me he has a job washing a car today, so I suggested he might want to get in practice by cleaning out ours first." Her voice sounded tight, and Josie wondered if the "practice" was intended to be punishment, or if it had just worked out that way.

The garage door was open, and all the doors of the Finch's aging blue Volvo stood open. A canister vacuum was plugged into the wall socket, the hose reaching into the car, but it wasn't running. Beau was nowhere in sight.

Josie left the garage and looked up and down the street. No Beau. The passageway door to the backyard was locked, so Josie peeked through the grimy window. Still no Beau. She returned to the garage and leaned on the trunk of the car to wait.

In the quiet she could hear a small sound. It was something between a wheeze and a squeak.

"Beau?" Josie said.

The sound came again. This time it sounded more like a snuffle. Josie walked around the car and peered in. Just visible in the half-light, crumpled in the back seat, was Beau. His face was buried in his knees, and his shoulders were heaving.

"Beau?" Josie said again.

Beau lifted a hand and waved it at her, as if to say "go away."

Josie climbed into the back seat of the Volvo and sat down. She didn't speak; she just sat there while Beau's shoulders continued to heave and he made muffled squeaks and snuffles. After what seemed like a very long time, he grew quieter.

"What happened?" Josie asked.

Beau gave a hiccup, then picked up the tail of his shirt and wiped his face with it. Josie could see him for the first time, and he was a wreck. His right eye was swollen nearly shut, and a pale bluish cast covered his cheekbone and part of the eyelid. The rest of his face was all red and white blotches, as it had been that day at Rossi Pool.

"She did it," Beau said. "Mom said she won't give me any money toward the skateboard and that if I keep fighting she won't even let me buy it with my own money. I don't think I'll ever get that skateboard, Josie. Not until I'm a very old man. Did you ever see an old man on a skateboard?"

"Did you explain it to her?" Josie asked. "Did you tell her that you tried to get away but that Matt Ventura caught up with you anyway?"

"I tried," Beau said, "but she still won't listen. She just said the same old things—like she'd never heard of just one person having a fight and that she thought I was out of control because my dad is away."

"That's dumb," Josie said. "Matt Ventura doesn't have anything to do with your father."

"That's what I told her. Then I said did it ever occur to her that Matt Ventura is the one who is out of control, not me. That was a mistake. She started to yell and said she wasn't going to have my father come home next month and find that his son had turned into a sociopath. It was strange, but I got the feeling she thinks my father would blame her for my fights."

"Wow," Josie said. "Your mother sure is doing some complicated thinking these days. I'll tell you, Beau—sometimes I think she reads too many books."

"Or not enough," Beau said. He sniffed loudly and wiped his nose down his sleeve. "The thing is, I really wish that my dad were here. I have a feeling he'd be giving me tips on fighting instead of punishing me. I said that to my mom."

"And what did she say?"

"She just said, 'Beau, your father is a peace-loving man,' in this very cold voice. I mean, I know he believes in peace and doesn't approve of fighting and all that. But somehow I have the idea he also doesn't believe you should get yourself pulverized."

"Probably not," Josie said. Getting pulverized sounded stupid to her under any circumstances.

She and Beau sat in silence for a while. "So what are you going to do?" she asked at last.

"Vacuum the car, I guess," Beau said. "I can't think of anything else. I don't see any way I'm ever going to get my skateboard now, and I should probably go to Skeet and get my money back. A deck is no good without the rest of the stuff, and it will be years before I can afford it all myself."

"Well, maybe it's not hopeless," Josie offered. "It might take a little longer, but you could still get it."

"Years longer," Beau said. "Besides, I know my mother. And the next time Matt Ventura punches me out, she's going to say I can't have a skateboard at all, no matter who pays for it. Trust me, it's hopeless." He got out of the car, switched on the overhead garage light, and started the vacuum.

Josie hung around and watched Beau vacuum the Volvo. Sometimes she just leaned against a post and watched, and sometimes she paced. She felt all wormy inside with feelings. She was mad at Paula Finch for one thing, and it was the first time she could remember being truly angry at Beau's mother.

And Josie felt bad for Beau. Worse than bad, nearly sick. Even though she thought a skateboard was a slightly silly thing to want so desperately, she understood how much it meant to Beau. She had wanted her bicycle the same way before she got it—almost as though she wanted it not only with her mind but with her whole body, even her toes.

Josie paced more and thought harder. There had to be an answer. Beau really *needed* that skateboard, and she wanted to help him get it. If only she could think of a way . . .

"Beau!" Josie leaped for the vacuum and switched it off. "I've got it! An idea! And it's brilliant. Well . . . maybe not brilliant, but it just might work."

Beau sat down on the edge of the front seat of the car and looked at her. "I'm listening," he said. "I'm desperate; I'll listen to anything."

"Okay," Josie said, "here goes: You tell your mother that it hasn't been Matt Ventura who was beating you up all this time. You tell her it was me!"

"How would *that* help?" Beau asked.

"Just shut up and listen," Josie said. "See, you have to make it sound like a confession. You tell her I've been acting really crazy lately and punching you out for practically no reason at all. And you say you didn't tell her sooner because you didn't want to get me in trouble. Right away you get points there for being loyal, see."

"But . . ."

"Quiet. Then you also tell her that of course you couldn't fight back because I'm not only your best friend but I'm a girl. You wouldn't want to hit a girl, would you?"

"No, but . . ."

"Of course not," Josie said. Since Beau was showing recent signs of becoming a sexist, it was more certain than ever that he wouldn't hit a girl! "Anyway, since you wouldn't hurt a girl, that would explain why I haven't had any black eyes or anything.

You get even more points that way for being . . . what's that *C* word? . . . chivalrous!"

Beau groaned.

Josie loved it. It wasn't just a good idea. The thought of Beau being chivalrous made it positively romantic! "Then you tell her that you've been trying to work things out with me yourself, so we can be friends without me belting you all the time. She's bound to appreciate that. It's a nonviolent solution."

"I don't know . . ." Beau said.

"Just give it a while to sink in," Josie said. "It's really perfect, you'll see."

"But suppose she won't buy it?"

"Oh, she'll have to buy it, because if she wants to check she can just ask me and I'll tell her the same thing. And your mother really likes me, Beau, so she'd believe it if both of us told her."

"Jeez, Josie, I don't know. It sounds chancy to me."

"It's not," Josie said. "Trust me." She was pacing back and forth rapidly now, rubbing her hands together. She felt positively inspired. "Anyhow, what have you got to lose, Beau?"

"Nothing, I guess, now that you put it that way." He paused. "I'll think about it, Josie. But thanks, though. That's really nice of you."

"Don't thank me," Josie said. "Just say yes. Think if you want to, but think fast. I'll wait right here." She climbed on the hood of the car and sat cross-legged, her arms folded across her chest. She did not intend to budge until Beau had agreed.

Beau turned the vacuum back on and went to work. He finished the back seat, then went to work on the front seat. He vacuumed the floors as well as the upholstery. He even vacuumed the ashtray, although nobody in his family smoked. Then he turned off the vacuum and wrapped up the cord.

"Okay," he said at last. "I'll do it. It's crazy, but it just might work."

"Great!" Josie grabbed Beau's hand and gave it a firm shake.

"And thanks, Josie. You're really a pal, you know that?"

Josie smiled. She knew. She wondered if he was thinking of marrying her right this minute.

"Oh, hey," Beau said, looking at his watch, "I've got to go. That guy's expecting me to be there to wash his car." He closed the doors to the Volvo, picked up the vacuum cleaner, and turned off the light. Josie followed him out and pulled down the garage door behind them.

"Let me know what happens," Josie said.

"Of course," he said. "It'll probably be later today because of my jobs, but I'll come let you know as soon as I can." He paused. Then, "Josie?"

"Yes?"

"Uh . . ." Beau hesitated, as though he had forgotten what he wanted to say—or had thought better of it. "Oh, nothing . . . just, well, thanks, that's all."

"You're welcome," Josie said.

Sandy and Bill Pucinski were seated at the dining

table when Josie came in. Bill was writing a major grocery list, and Sandy was making a list of errands.

"You're coming with me," Josie's mother said to her. "We need to shop for a few clothes for you. I hope you've given some thought to what you need."

"Oh, don't worry," Josie said. "I've thought." She ran to her room for her list, folded it carefully, and put it in her pocket for the right moment.

The right moment came when they had stepped off the escalator at the discount clothing store. Josie handed the list to her mother.

"What's this?" her mother shrieked.

"My list."

"Some list! This is two full pages long, Josie."

"It's not really as much as it seems," Josie said. "Lots of those things are just socks, you'll notice. It's just that I listed the colors separately to go with the different-colored outfits." None of the colors listed was green.

"We're not buying 'outfits,' Josie. We're buying a few clothes. Enough to tide you over, that's all."

"To tide me over until what?" Josie asked. Did her mother expect her to reach a certain height and then start shrinking?

"Until later. You certainly don't need all of these things now. Like this item, for instance." Sandy Pucinski read, " 'Very slinky dress, red or black.' Or 'high heels with thin straps and rhinestones embedded

94

in heels.' No twelve-year-old girl needs clothes like that."

"Well, I might," Josie said. "Anyway, I know you hate to shop, so I thought we should get it all over with at once."

"When the day comes that you need a slinky dress, Josie Pucinski, I'll bring you back. Or you can come by yourself; you'll be old enough to drive by then. And you also don't need ten pair of underwear in ten different colors. That's absurd. The underwear you have still fits you. You didn't grow out of that."

"No," Josie said, "but I didn't think you'd want me wearing raggedy old underwear under all those nice new clothes."

"I think I'll survive," he mother said. "Now come with me. We'll find some nice sturdy jeans and maybe a sweater or two—something large and durable."

"Ugh," Josie said. "Sensible clothes." She followed her mother to the section labeled Sportswear—Misses.

Evidently her mother had forgotten what it was like to be twelve years old. Or else she had never had Josie's problems. But it was a cinch that no boy would ever look at Josie as long as she continued to resemble an understuffed scarecrow. The boys at school liked girls who looked like girls—the ones who had large breasts or pretty clothes. And unless a miracle happened, clothes were Josie's only hope. Her mother's idea of style was not going to help.

By five o'clock she and Josie had agreed on exactly

two items: a pair of white cotton slacks, pegged, and an oversize aqua shirt made out of some kind of fabric that imitated silk. Josie wondered why Kim had never mentioned that clothes shopping was such a struggle.

At home Josie tried the clothes on again, over the same old underwear. "Hey," she said to her reflection in the mirror, "you're not Madonna, but at least you look more like a girl than an it."

By five forty-five Josie was beginning to get antsy. Beau still hadn't reported back. She was on the point of ringing the bell to the Finch flat herself when the knock finally came at her door.

"Come outside," Beau said. He was wearing a slightly lopsided grin.

Josie closed the front door behind her and went to sit at the bottom of the front steps with Beau.

"Well?" she said.

"It worked," Beau said.

"All *right*!" Josie slapped him five.

"I don't know, though, Josie—I'm still worried."

"Whatever for?" she asked. "It worked, didn't it? Your mother is going to help pay for the skateboard now, isn't she?"

"Yeah, that part's okay. She said she'd help. . . ."

"I knew it! I just knew it would work!"

"But it was so easy," Beau said. "It makes me nervous when something is *that* easy."

"It was supposed to be easy, Beau. A brilliant idea wouldn't be too brilliant if it was hard."

"I suppose you're right," he said. Then he paused. "There was one small hitch, though."

"What?" Josie asked brightly. No problem was insurmountable now that they had come this far.

"Well, you know how my mother is lately. She said she hoped you weren't turning into a troubled child. She said maybe it's too big a burden for you to have a talented sister like Kim." Beau looked embarrassed.

"Good grief," Josie said. "What did you say to that?"

"I just told her the part about how I was trying to work things out with you myself, so I think it's okay. She said she was sure I could persuade you that talking was more productive than hitting. Her words: more productive."

Josie laughed. "Okay, I'm persuaded," she said. "There, see how easy that was?"

They sat on the steps a while longer, not saying much, just watching the occasional car go by and picking up tiny pieces of gravel and chucking them toward the street.

"By the way," Beau said, "I got five bucks for washing that guy's car today."

"Great!" Josie said.

Beau picked up another piece of gravel and chucked it toward the road. Then he picked up another piece and bounced it in the palm of his hand. "You know what, Josie?"

"What?" Josie said.

"Well . . . it's just that I used to be in love with you in third grade. I didn't tell you before now because it's sort of embarrassing, but I thought you'd like to know."

"Oh. Well, thanks," Josie said. She smiled.

"Of course that was way back in third grade," Beau added hastily. "I'm not anymore, you understand."

"Of course not," Josie said.

"We're just old friends. Almost like best friends, but more like pals, know what I mean?"

Josie sighed. She looked down at her new aqua shirt and white slacks. She might as well have come to this conversation in a green potato sack. Just old friends . . .

"Beau?" she said.

"Huh?"

"You need to learn when to shut up."

Chapter Nine

Summer began to get old for Josie. She discovered that it didn't necessarily take three months to grow tired of vacation. It could happen in a hurry. For Josie it had taken less than a week. When school let out in June, she would have sworn that nothing could ever make her want to go back. But now, no more than six weeks later, she found herself thinking that it might be interesting to be in a science class.

First there were the swimming lessons. Even though Josie had improved by attaching herself to Cathy's class, there seemed to be a limit to how much progress she could make. She still had trouble with rhythmic breathing, and she knew that real swimmers had to keep it going. What would she do if she ended up at a camp where there was no shallow water?

Josie concluded that what she really needed was lessons in treading water. After all, if the purpose of learning how to swim was to be able to save your own life, then treading water was all that was needed. Unless, of course, there was someplace you wanted to swim *to*. But the more Josie thought about it, the more she was convinced that there wasn't anyplace she wanted to go that you'd get to by swimming. Like Great America, for instance. You'd take a car to get there. And even if you wanted to go to Hawaii, you'd never swim; you'd take a plane.

So Josie decided that her efforts should be concentrated on learning to tread water. A girl in her class already knew how, and she showed Josie. But when Josie tried it, her toes scraped on the bottom of the pool. Some days long legs were more of a hindrance than a help.

One day Josie walked up to Don and asked, "When do we get to learn how to tread water?"

"As soon as you can swim across the deep end of the pool," Don said.

Josie looked at him suspiciously. "Is that your rule or the pool's rule?" she asked. It was possible that Don was trying to cover up for not knowing how to teach swimming.

"It's everybody's rule," he answered. "You have to be able to swim in case you go under."

Josie started to ask what a lifeguard was for, but Don's jaw had gone all slack again, and Josie felt he had probably told her everything he knew. She dressed and went home.

Home was another problem. For several days after Beau had hatched Josie's plot, Paula Finch acted strangely around Josie. She still called Josie "cutie," but she also looked at her quizzically, as though Josie had grown an extra nose but Paula was too polite to mention it.

Then, even when Paula seemed to relax and behave normally, there was the problem of Beau. He still wouldn't go out except to walk Mrs. Sloane's dog, and Josie was sick of being cooped up. They had played Trivial Pursuit for three or four days, by which time Josie never wanted to see it again. Then Josie had bought them each a copy of *Games*, which they did for two more days. Then on Wednesday they had played hearts and crazy eights.

"This is just like when we had chicken pox," Josie said, during the second game of crazy eights. "Except we don't itch." The suit was hearts, and Josie had just drawn three spades in a row.

"And except for the baking soda baths," Beau said. "Don't forget about them."

"Those were for you," Josie said. "I didn't have baking soda baths, because I didn't get chicken pox in certain places . . . which I won't name."

"Thanks," Beau said. He put down another heart. He must have had every heart in the deck. "It's not as if I got to choose, though. Chicken pox do their own thing. They don't ask permission."

Josie was losing heavily. She had all spades and diamonds, and none of them in the right denominations. She hadn't won a card game all afternoon, and she was in the mood to be better than Beau at something. A case of chicken pox in fourth grade was the best she could come up with on short notice.

"I guess some people are luckier at chicken pox than others," she said, trying for a haughty tone of voice. She drew from the pile again. A diamond. Then another spade. Then a three of hearts, which she put down.

"Yeah," Beau grinned. "Some people are lucky at pox, and some are lucky at cards." He put down a queen of hearts, his last card. "I win. The nice thing is that you can only get chicken pox once, Josie, but you can win at cards over and over."

Josie went home. In her room she sat at her desk and got out a piece of paper. At the top she wrote:

Things I Can Do Without Beau
1. Ride different bus lines around the city.
   (Rate them for scenery on a scale of 1-10)
   (Rate the drivers for courtesy and cheerfulness)
2. Go into every store on Clement Street between Arguello and Tenth Avenue.
3. Get a pen pal in Australia.
   (Ask her if she skis in summer)
4. Go to Academy of Sciences. Volunteer for job feeding the dolphins.
5. Dial own phone number in different area codes.
   (Ask who lives there)

6. Clean room.

(Do this only if bored to *death* and
absolutely desperate)

After swimming on Thursday, Josie walked to the corner of Arguello and Balboa. When the No. 31 Balboa came, Josie got on it. She sat in the seat right behind the driver. Ordinarily the seats near the driver were for handicapped and old people, but the bus was nearly empty. Besides, Josie couldn't very well rate the drivers from the back of the bus.

She placed the bag with her soggy swim suit on the floor between her feet and got out her notebook. She wrote the name of the bus, then she wrote the name and number of the driver.

Mitchell was the driver's name. She watched him carefully. He never spoke to anyone unless they asked a question. He never smiled. He lurched the bus before people had taken their seats. Josie gave Mitchell a two for courtesy and a one for cheerfulness. She gave the bus route a three because there was one nice view from the top of a hill and because it ended at the Ferry Building.

On the way back she had a different driver. He lurched the bus too, but he sang all the time except for when he had to answer a question. Josie gave him a four for courtesy and a ten for cheerfulness.

Josie got off the bus at Park Presidio and boarded a No. 28. She gave the route an eight for scenery because it stopped at the Golden Gate Bridge and ended up at Fort Mason. The driver noticed her notebook and asked her what she was doing. "I'm rating you on courtesy and cheerfulness," she said. He didn't speak to her the rest of the way to Fort Mason. She gave him a zero for everything.

At home Josie could hear Kim in her room practicing her cello. She was trying to play along with a recording of an orchestra. Josie opened Kim's door and stuck her head in.

"Hi," she said.

"Shhhh," Kim said. She frowned, then reached over to her tape player and switched it off. "You ruined it," she said. "Now I have to start over."

Josie went into her own room and flopped on her bed. She stuck a finger in her mouth and wiggled her other loose molar. Soon, she thought. She wondered whether she should offer her father a two-for-one special. Since turning down her previous offer, he hadn't even mentioned her tooth. Josie might be stuck with her teeth from now on.

Tap. Tap, tap. Josie sat up. The tap came again. She looked around her room. The door was open, but nobody was there so it couldn't be that. She didn't have any pets, so a scratching dog was out. Tap, tap. A raccoon maybe? She'd heard that there were raccoons in the park and that sometimes they moved into neighborhoods to get garbage. But raccoons were supposed to be nocturnal. This was broad daylight.

Tap. Now Josie was sure—it came from the window. She got up and crossed the room. Hanging outside the window over Josie's desk was a clothespin attached to a piece of string. In the jaws of the clothespin was a folded piece of paper. It swung against the window with a tap.

"Beau!" Back in fourth grade, Beau had come up with the clothespin-on-a-string idea as a means of passing secret messages to one another through their bedroom windows. The trouble was, it was a flawed system. Beau could dangle a message down to Josie, but Josie couldn't dangle a message *up* to Beau. When they realized they didn't have any secrets anyway, they'd forgotten about it. A clothespin message from Beau was about the last thing Josie was expecting.

She opened the window and retrieved the paper. It was a sheet of binder paper with light blue lines. Beau's handwriting was scrawled across it diagonally. *TROUBLE!* it said. *Meet me in the old fort at 7:30. Don't tell anyone!!!*

Josie tore off a corner of the paper and wrote *Okay*. She clipped it back in the clothespin and tugged three times on the line. The clothespin slowly rose out of view.

It was Kim's turn to wash the dinner dishes that night, and when Josie came through the kitchen at seven thirty and said she felt like taking out the trash, Kim just said, "Uh-huh," as though it was the most normal thing in the world.

Josie dropped the trash in the areaway can and let

herself out the door to the backyard. In the dark she made her way to the edge of the deck, then ducked under it.

"Are you here?" she whispered.

"Over here," came Beau's voice.

Josie groped along on her hands and knees until she reached the "lookout bench"—a board laid across two cinderblocks. She eased herself onto it cautiously, hoping any nearby spiders would run away before she touched them.

"What's wrong?" she asked.

"You'd know if you could see my face," Beau said.

"Your face? What does your face . . ." Then she got it. "Oh, no. You didn't have another fight with Matt Ventura, did you?"

"Yeah, but it wasn't really my fault, Josie. Honest. I was just minding my own business, coming out of a store, when Ventura jumped me."

"Let me guess," Josie said. "The store just happened to be on Clement Street, and it just happened to be called Skeet's Skates."

"Yes, but . . ."

"Beau, why did you go there? I thought you weren't going anyplace except to walk Conchita."

Beau sighed. "That's just the thing, see. I thought it was safe, just this once. Mrs. Sloane paid me nearly seven dollars, and I had my allowance and the money from the car washing, so I thought I'd just make a quick trip to Skeet's Skates and make a payment on my deck. This was the last payment on the deck, Josie. Now I can start on the trucks."

Josie groaned. "I don't know, Beau. If you're so determined to self-destruct, why don't you just invite Ventura to your house and get it over with? Or maybe he could come at regular intervals, say on Tuesday and Friday afternoons. That way you'd never quite have a chance to heal."

"Very funny, Josie. Anyway, it's no biggie. My mom said it will probably heal okay even without stitches. It's just a little cut over the eye. She used one of those butterfly closures you can buy in the store."

"Jeez . . ." Josie breathed. She wished they were sitting in the light. In her imagination Beau had a butterfly-shaped bandage that covered half of his face.

"But that's not why I got you down here," Beau said. "The trouble isn't my face, it's my mother."

"She's mad, right?"

"And how!"

"So she's not going to help pay for the skateboard?" Beau was right—he wasn't going to get that skateboard until he was a very, *very* old man.

"Well, no. That is, she didn't mention the skateboard, not a word. What she's mad about now is . . . well . . ." Beau sighed again. "You."

Josie's stomach lurched. "Me?" she said.

"Yes. See, she thinks you . . ."

"She thinks I hit you," Josie supplied.

107

"Well, yeah. I didn't *say* you did. It's just that now that's what she thinks."

This time it was Josie's turn to sigh. "I'm not surprised," she said. "I mean, that's what she was *supposed* to think, so it's not a big surprise that she does."

"I know," Beau said. He didn't sound happy.

"And she's mad?"

"Very."

"At me?" Josie said, as though asking again would make it go away.

"Yes."

Josie thought. Somehow, when she had come up with the scheme for getting Beau out of trouble, she hadn't envisioned getting herself *in* trouble. And the thought that Paula Finch was really angry at her— not just funny-acting, but really angry—gave Josie a sick feeling in the pit of her stomach.

Still, what could she do? The only way to get herself out of trouble now was to get Beau right back in it. And the scheme had, after all, been Josie's idea.

"When I was supposed to persuade you not to hit me anymore, we forgot about the important part," Beau said.

"Yeah," Josie said, "like who was going to persuade Matt Ventura."

"Right."

Josie dug the heel of her shoe into the dirt and shoved. She dragged it back and forth a few times. In a minute she could feel a groove beneath her foot.

"Okay, then," Josie said at last. "Your mother's mad at me, but I can live with that for a while. When you get your skateboard, maybe we can tell her the truth. But for now, she's just going to be mad."

"Very mad," Beau corrected.

"Very mad," Josie said. "But that's okay. I can handle it." She straightened out her spine and waited to get that noble feeling that came from doing something nice for someone at your own expense. It came, but it was on the puny side.

"I haven't told you the worst, though," Beau said.

"Oh, no. What?"

"The worst part is that I'm not allowed to play . . . well, hang out with you anymore."

"What! Oh, Beau, no! She can't do that!"

"She's doing it," Beau said. "I told her I thought it was crummy and mean and everything, Josie, but she has this idea that you have become dangerous or something. She was saying stuff like she thought your parents should have paid more attention to you before you got to be a troubled child. It was like she completely forgot that two weeks ago *I* was supposed to be the sociopath. And I couldn't talk her out of it, at least not without telling her the truth. And I didn't know what to do."

Josie felt a choking sensation in her throat. She wasn't sure whether she was on the verge of crying or yelling, but it was one of the two. Mostly she felt angry. Angry at Paula Finch. How could Paula think those things about her? She'd known Josie all her life. Couldn't she figure out that Josie would never really hurt Beau? Josie was incensed.

"Well, I think it stinks," she said. "Your mother can be mad at me if she wants, but I'm mad at her, too. In fact, I'm twice as mad at her as she is at me." However much *that* was.

"Don't you think we ought to tell her the truth?" Beau asked.

"No!" Josie said. "Well, yes. Maybe. Oh, Beau, I don't know. You know what happens if we tell her the truth."

"Good-bye skateboard," Beau said miserably.

"Right. And then she might still be angry at me anyway for cooking up this whole thing. So I don't know if we should or not." Part of Josie was so offended that she felt Paula Finch didn't *deserve* to know the truth. And another part wanted to go make an immediate confession. She mostly felt confused, full of anger and hurt, and couldn't tell what was important anymore. Beau's skateboard . . .

"I don't know, Beau. I really don't. You decide. We'll do whatever you want."

"I don't know, either," Beau said. "I mean, I really want that skateboard, Josie. But I'm not wild about lying to my mother, even if she is being unreasonable. And it doesn't seem right to get you in trouble. So we can tell her the truth if you want. It's okay."

110

Josie had the sensation that Beau had left something out. It ran around the edges of her mind for a minute; then it came to her: Beau had not said he would miss being with Josie if they couldn't be together anymore. He thought it was wrong to get her in trouble, but he wouldn't actually miss Josie. Not like he'd miss his skateboard, that was for sure. Josie gulped.

"No," she said. "I don't want you to lose your skateboard, Beau. So let your mother think what she wants about me. It's no skin off my nose." The lump in Josie's throat had become boulder-size.

"Are you sure, Josie?" Beau's voice was subdued.

"I'm sure."

"Well . . . okay. But Josie, we'll tell her the truth just as soon as I get my skateboard, okay? Then she won't be mad anymore."

But I might, Josie thought.

Josie shoved her foot back and forth in the dirt some more. She made a really deep groove. She hoped Beau wouldn't fall in it on his way out.

At last Josie said, "You know what would be really good, Beau? It would be good if you could get Ventura to lay off. Then we wouldn't have any problems at all."

"I know," Beau said. "I'm working on it."

Back inside her flat, Josie went to the living room and turned on the television. She was in the mood for something completely different—something that wasn't about skateboards or angry mothers or aspiring thugs with tattoos. A sitcom would be nice, or a game show where everyone jumped up and down and hugged each other.

Josie punched her way through all the channels. On every single station someone was shooting at someone else with a gun.

She turned off the TV and went to bed.

Chapter Ten

Josie awoke with a pop on Saturday morning. She had the feeling that this was a special day, though at first she couldn't think why.

Then she remembered. She slumped back on her pillow. This was her first day of being persona non grata in the Finch household.

Now what was she going to do? It was one thing to decide to strike out on her own because playing cards and board games with Beau had grown stale. But it was quite another to be told she couldn't play with Beau even if she wanted to.

And it was all her own fault, she knew that. If it hadn't been for her big idea about helping Beau out, she could still be with him any time she wanted. But that's what friends were for, wasn't it? To help each other out?

On the other hand, what good was it to have a friend you couldn't see anymore? When she thought about it, what good was Beau, period? When was the last time he had done something Josie had wanted to do, like go ice-skating? In fact, when was the last time Beau had paid any real attention to her at all? She wasn't even a girl to him. If Beau ever thought about girls at all, Josie was pretty sure he never thought of her in that category. The only thing he thought about anymore was that stupid skateboard and making money to buy it. If Josie were a skateboard, then he would pay attention to her.

Josie looked down at the shape she made stretched out beneath the bedclothes. It was a formless shape, more like a pole than a person. The only clue that there was someone alive under the covers was her feet making a small twin-peaked mountain near the end of the bed. Everything else was flat and straight. Josie wondered whether Beau failed to notice her simply because he was so used to her, or whether it was because she was a stupid-looking girl. Maybe Beau was right—it might be an improvement to be a skateboard.

Or it would be easier to be Kim—to be short and talented, and have boyfriends and a big bedroom, and have your entire life figured out from the time you were seven years old.

The only thing certain in Josie's life was that it was now a bright, sunny Saturday morning in the middle of summer, and Josie's one good friend was off limits.

"So what are you going to do about it, Josie Pucinski?" she said aloud.

She reached in her mouth and gave a hard yank to her loose tooth. It came free in her hand.

Josie sat up and studied the tooth closely. It was perfect. Not a mark on it anywhere. If the Tooth Prince weren't so hard to do business with, he'd pay a lot of money for a tooth in this condition. And if Josie had a lot of money . . .

That was it. With a lot of money, Josie could help Beau pay for his skateboard sooner. Then they could be friends again. *If*, that is, Beau was worth it—which Josie hadn't quite decided.

But the first thing, she figured, was to get the money. After that, she could decide whether to spend it on Beau . . . or, say, those rhinestone heels.

Josie rinsed her mouth in the bathroom. Then she went to her mother's sewing cabinet for another piece of black velvet. She used the first star as a pattern for the second. Then she got dressed and brushed her hair.

Her parents were seated at the dining table when Josie arrived. Bill was reading the business section of the paper, and Sandy was reading the front section. Kim sat between them, nibbling on a piece of toast.

Josie set the two velvet stars on the dining table, smack in the middle. Then she set a tooth in the center of each star.

"*Josie*," Kim said. "Yecch!"

Sandy Pucinski looked up from the paper. "Josie," she said, "why on earth did you bring those things in here?"

"They're for decoration," Josie said. "I had them

on my bureau, but I realized I should bring them out here where the whole family can enjoy them. It's less selfish that way. Aren't they gorgeous?"

Bill Pucinski put down his paper. "I'm not sure gorgeous is the right word," he said. "Another word might do better. Like grotesque . . . or ghoulish."

"Are you saying these aren't beautiful teeth?" Josie asked. "Is there something wrong with my teeth?"

"Well, no," her mother said, "but . . ."

"I mean if there's something wrong with my teeth, then I think you should say so. Maybe we could do something about them. We could have them capped, for instance. Movie stars have their teeth capped, and they all have beautiful teeth." Josie leered around the table, making sure everyone got a good look at her teeth.

"There is nothing wrong with your teeth," her father said. "And we are not going to spend twenty-four thousand dollars having them capped."

"Then if there's nothing wrong with them, why can't I leave these here?" Josie asked. "I think you should make up your minds."

"Well . . ." her mother said.

"Mom, *Dad* . . ." Kim said, "she *can't* leave them on the table. Keith is coming to visit today. What would he think?"

"Josie," her mother said, "the table is really not the appropriate place for your teeth, even though they are quite beautiful, as you pointed out."

"Oh." Josie considered. "Maybe you're right.

Maybe this isn't the very best place for them."

"Good," her father said.

"Somebody might set a casserole dish on one if I leave them here. So I think I'll just put them on the mantelpiece. Or better yet, on the coffee table!"

"*Mom* . . ." Kim wailed.

"Or," Josie went on, "I could maybe use some cardboard to stiffen the backs of the stars, and a dab of rubber cement to hold the teeth in place, and *hang* them. In the foyer. So you can see them right as you come in the front door."

"Bill, I think I hear the distant flutter of Tooth Fairy wings," Sandy Pucinski said. "I suggest you do something. Now." She looked determined.

"Okay, okay," Bill Pucinski said. "I'll buy them. But I want everyone at this table to know this is extortion."

"Just buy the teeth," Kim said. "Lecture her later."

Josie smiled. "Ten dollars apiece sounds good to me," she said. "But I'll give you a special two-for-one rate of fifteen dollars. Plus, I'll write you a thank-you note in honor of your contribution to a worthy cause."

"That's outrageous!" her father said.

"Bargain with her," Sandy Pucinski said. "I don't care how long it takes, just get those teeth." She picked up her coffee cup and went into the kitchen.

"Two dollars fifty cents," Bill Pucinski said.

"Apiece?"

Her father took a deep breath. "All right, apiece."

"That's five dollars, right?"

"Yes. Two-fifty twice is still five dollars, I believe." He sounded irritated.

"Five dollars sounds nice," Josie said. "Each."

"*Each*? That's ten dollars! That's highway robbery! Never."

Josie imagined she could see thin wisps of smoke rising from her father's ears. "Tell you what," she said. "We'll split the difference, just because I'm a nice person. Seven-fifty for the pair."

"Seven-fifty . . ." her father sputtered.

"And that's my final offer," Josie said. She reached for the stars and pulled them toward her.

"Sold!" her father said hastily. He stood up and pulled his wallet from his back pocket. "Josie Pucinski, I do believe you're turning into a hustler."

"Is that a talent?" Josie asked.

Kim let out a little laugh, but quickly clapped her hand over her mouth.

"No, but it generally helps if you want to lead a life of crime." A smile began to form around the edges of Bill Pucinski's mouth.

"Well, right now I'm just a fund raiser," Josie said. She held out her hand as her father counted the money. "But I'm working on the life of crime."

Keith arrived in the early afternoon. He turned out to have muscles, just as Bill Pucinski had said. He also turned out to bear a strong resemblance to Yo-Yo Ma. Josie wondered what it was about Keith that Kim liked best.

When Keith excused himself to wash up before dinner, Sandy Pucinski said, "He's cute, Kim."

"I know," Kim said. She sounded serene.

"He has good manners," Bill Pucinski said. He sounded grudging.

Josie liked Keith. Over dinner she gazed at him and wondered whether, if she were seventeen years old like Kim, she would trade Beau in for Keith.

Kim and Keith talked about a movie they were planning to see that evening. It starred Meryl Streep, who happened to be one of Josie's idols.

"Boy, I sure wish I could see that," Josie said.

Keith looked up from his lamb chop. "Why don't you come along?" he said. "There's always room for one more."

"I don't know . . ." Sandy Pucinski said.

"No!" Kim said. "That is, I think it's R-rated. It's not for little kids."

Josie was stung. "I'm not a little kid! And anyhow, I know all about what goes on in those movies. I mean, I know all about *it*, so it's not as if I'm going to be corrupted or anything."

The truth was that Josie knew very little about *it*. But she knew enough to know that if you pretended to be well informed, people began saying things in front of you that you otherwise wouldn't hear.

"I don't know," Bill Pucinski said. "I'm not sure I want you going to R-rated movies yet, Josie."

"I don't think there's any real nudity in it, Mr.

Pucinski," Keith said. "My sister saw it, and she's thirteen years old."

"Please, Dad?" Josie said.

"Kim?" Bill Pucinski asked.

"I'm outnumbered," Kim said. "I give up." She looked at Keith and smiled. Josie had the idea they were holding hands under the table.

"Yea!" Josie said. Then she added, "By the way, Keith, I'm embarking on a life of crime. For a dollar I'll sit two rows ahead of you and Kim."

"*Josie!*" Sandy, Bill, and Kim said in unison.

"Never mind," Josie said. "Joke."

By the time Keith left on Sunday afternoon, they had begun to think of him as a member of the family. He even hugged Josie good-bye, and Bill Pucinski shook his hand and said, "I look forward to seeing you again." It sounded sincere.

Josie found Kim in her bedroom later, writing a letter.

"Keith's nice," Josie said.

"Yes, he is," Kim said.

"Is he coming back?"

"Yes, no thanks to you, Josie."

"Keith *liked* me," Josie protested.

"Well, that's true. But really, Josie, you should check with me first before you start going on my dates with me."

"Okay." She watched Kim write Keith's name on the front of an envelope. "Is Keith a member of a Chinese gang?" Josie asked.

"No!" Kim laughed. "Where did you get an idea like that?"

"Well, it's just that he looks so tough, with all those muscles, even though he's actually nice."

"Well, in the first place he's Japanese-American, not Chinese. Yashida is a Japanese name. And in the second place he's a third-generation pacifist. And in the third place, the muscles are for throwing discus, not street fighting," Kim said.

"Pacifists are the ones who don't fight, right?" Josie asked, checking.

"Right," Kim said.

"So what does he do if someone wants to fight with *him*?" Josie asked. "Does he just stand there and get punched out, or does he fight back?"

"I have no idea; you'd have to ask him." Kim opened a desk drawer and pulled out a sheet of stamps.

"But suppose a bully was just determined to fight with him," Josie persisted. "What then?"

"I still don't know," Kim said. "I do know that it's very complicated when a pacifist meets up with a bully, but I don't know how it gets resolved."

"Neither do I," Josie said. "But I'd sure like to find out."

She turned to leave Kim's room. Then she had another thought. "Is Keith related to Yo-Yo Ma?" she asked.

"No," Kim laughed. "Yo-Yo Ma *is* Chinese. Really, Josie, you're going to have to learn to tell the difference before we let you out in polite society."

Chapter Eleven

"Laps!" Don yelled from the side of Rossi Pool.

Josie pushed off smoothly and began stroking across the pool. That was another thing she had learned from watching Cathy's class: you should push off smoothly, not leap in the air and flop onto the water. Josie was getting quicker starts now that she didn't belly-flop.

Halfway across the pool, Josie stopped to catch her breath. She still couldn't get the hang of rhythmic breathing. Most likely she never would. "Courage," she said to herself and dug back into the water.

Courage. That was what Beau had written on a note Josie found dangling in front of her bedroom window when she got up this morning. That was all it said *Courage*, in bright red marker. The note was damp from the morning dew, and Josie thought Beau might have lowered it on the clothespin the night before.

For reasons she could not explain, the note pleased Josie. She folded it and tucked it under her pillow.

Later in the morning there had been another note. This one said, *Mom leaving for school at nine-thirty. Come up for cards.*

Maybe it was the combination of the two notes, but Josie suddenly felt that Beau might be worth all the trouble after all. Or at least some of it. He did miss her, it seemed. At least he thought of her often enough to send messages.

At nine forty-five, Josie went upstairs to the Finch flat. She was relieved to see that in the daylight Beau's butterfly bandage was relatively small.

"I'm going to help pay for your skateboard," Josie said. "I already have seven-fifty I got for some teeth, and I'm going to ask for a raise in my allowance." She had thought this over. She would keep her regular allowance and save the extra for Beau. Then she could still buy the occasional bean cake.

"No," Beau said. "You've helped enough. It's nice of you, but paying for the skateboard is my job. Forget it, Josie."

Josie left for her swimming lesson feeling better about Beau but worse about everything else. She'd had to sneak to see her best friend. Somehow that didn't seem right. Still, she was more determined than ever to help him earn some money to pay for his skateboard. She just wouldn't tell him until she had earned enough, that was all.

"Courage," she said to herself again, and plunged back into the water at Rossi Pool. She slogged her way through two more laps, then stopped to rest again. Cathy's group was at the deep end of the pool. They had edged their way carefully into the deep water, holding onto the gutter, and now, one at a time, they were learning to tread water. Cathy was in the water, and one by one she eased the kids into the open water and showed them how to wave their arms and scissor their legs. Josie watched as Cathy worked with the last girl in the row. She seemed to catch on quickly, and in a minute Josie could see her laughing.

Josie made a decision. She turned and swam in quick, choppy strokes back to the side of the pool and hauled herself out. Don was standing with his back to the pool, talking with the lifeguard. Josie tapped him on the back.

"Hey," he said, turning. "You're supposed . . ."

"I quit," Josie said. She turned and walked toward the locker room.

"Hey, wait," Don called. "I need your name. If you're going to quit, I have to know who you are." He reached for his clipboard.

"Wrong," Josie said. "You needed to know my name to teach me how to swim. For quitting, you can just guess."

As Josie walked down Arguello Boulevard, her wet swim suit flapping against her leg in its plastic bag, she had a bad moment. Maybe quitting had been a mistake. What if you had to be certified in swimming to get into a summer camp? No, surely not. Camps had swimming instructors, too. And any one of them was bound to be better than Don. She would take her chances with the South Fork of the Toulomne River. And she'd take her chances with her parents, too. She hadn't asked their permission to quit, so she'd just have to explain it so they could understand.

Josie spent the early afternoon "doing" Clement Street. She went into every store on the south side of the street, and most on the north side. She counted, in all, three places you could buy flowers, four for getting your film developed, seventeen restaurants, one movie theater, two picture-framing shops, two bookstores, a fish market, a welding shop, and five places you could buy shoes.

Josie avoided the welding shop. She had the idea you should bring the front end of a truck if you went in there, and she was short on trucks. But in most stores Josie took her time and looked around—browsing, her mother would call it. In three shops Josie found mailing lists on the counters. She wrote her name and address on these. It always made her feel important to get mail, even if it was only advertising.

In the Stubby Pencil, Josie bought four sheets of paper-by-the-pound and two envelopes. She planned to use them to write to her pen pal, as soon as she got one.

In Woolworth's she spent a lot of time at the cosmetics counter. Josie wasn't sure she was old enough to wear makeup yet, but she was old enough to think about it. It was hard to tell what the right look would be. Should she buy lip gloss? Colored or clear? Eye shadow? Were you supposed to buy eye shadow to match your eyes or your clothes? And there were dozens of different kinds of mascara. Some said they would make your lashes longer. Others said they were guaranteed waterproof (a good idea if you were crying), or were good for people with allergies.

Josie noticed that a lady in a Woolworth's smock was hovering near her. She was restocking the displays but spent almost as much time looking at Josie. Soon Josie began to feel uneasy. Did the woman think Josie might steal something?

As soon as she thought she might have been mistaken for a shoplifter, Josie began to feel guilty. Had the woman listened in on her most secret thoughts? Did she know that Josie, if she were absolutely all alone in the store and certain there was no way of ever being found out, *might* take something? Would probably at least consider it?

Guiltily, Josie picked up a bottle of coral-colored nail polish and a box of press-on fingernails. She took them to the counter and paid for them.

It was only when she was out on the sidewalk again that Josie realized her mistake. She didn't want the fingernails or the nail polish. In fact, if she could have stolen them, she still wouldn't have wanted them.

Josie walked home feeling defeated. Probably it

was her new life as a hustler, a liar, and a hatcher of plots that had made her buy things she didn't want. Once you're a criminal, she thought, you walk around feeling like a criminal. And that leads to having to prove that you're *not* a criminal.

At home Josie sat at her desk with the stationery spread in front of her. She chewed on the end of a ballpoint pen for a few minutes, then began to write:

Dear Pen Pal,

How is Australia? It is summer here, so it must be winter there. What I want to know is whether you *call* it winter, or do you just call it summer even though it's snowing? And do you go to school now, or are you on summer vacation like me? I think it would be strange to have summer vacation in January.

I am twelve years old and I don't have a boyfriend yet. Do you? I am also very tall, which may have something to do with not having a boyfriend.

Otherwise, I am just a normal girl. I don't do drugs and I don't steal.

Please write.

Love,
Josie Pucinski

Josie sealed the letter in an envelope. Then she realized she had forgotten her question about skiing. Well, there would be time for that later.

She opened the box of press-on fingernails and spread them on her bed. The directions said you should trim the bottoms to the shape of your own nails, so Josie got a small pair of scissors and began snipping away. When they were all trimmed, she peeled the adhesive off the back and stuck them on her own fingernails. Then she opened the coral nail polish and began painting them.

The nails were bright. Very bright. And long. Including the nail, Josie's middle finger was six inches long. It was awesome.

"I smell nail polish," Kim said. She set her cello case in the doorway of Josie's room, took off her sweatshirt, and draped it over the top of the case.

Josie held her hands up and wriggled the fingers. "What do you think?" she asked.

"Ick," Kim said. She sat next to Josie and took a closer look. "No offense, Josie, but those are really gross."

"You don't think they're glamorous?" Josie stretched her arm to display them from a distance.

"They're awful," Kim said flatly.

"Hmmm," Josie said. She studied them a bit longer. "I think I'll keep them on for a while anyway. Maybe they look better once you're used to them."

"Nobody could get used to those," Kim said. "And I think you should take them off before Mom has a fit. She got home at the same time I did, and she's in a rotten mood."

"I don't know *how* to get them off," Josie said. "And besides, I'm not ready yet."

Kim returned to her cello case and picked it up. "Well, if I were you, I'd get ready soon because Mom wants to see you. And from the sound of her voice I think you're in hot water with her."

"Uh-oh," Josie said.

"What have you been up to, anyway? Is it something they'll hang you for?"

"That depends on which thing I'm in trouble for," Josie said. She folded her hands behind her back and left her room.

Sandy Pucinski sat slumped on the couch. Her shoes were off, her feet on the coffee table, and her eyes were closed. A stranger would think she was asleep, but Josie knew better.

"Mom?" she said softly.

"I'm getting a headache," her mother said.

"That's what I thought," Josie said.

"And I'm not in a very good mood."

"I thought that, too," Josie said.

"Plus, I'm very, very disappointed in you, Josie Pucinski."

"Me too," Josie said. She wasn't sure yet which of her several crimes her mother was on to, but experience had taught her that things went easier if you just confessed to everything right away.

"I just ran into Paula Finch," her mother said.

"Oh." Josie gulped.

Sandy Pucinski opened her eyes and looked straight at Josie. "Paula had quite a tale to tell, young lady. She says you've been beating up Beau. For *weeks*, she tells me. I could hardly believe it."

"It is sort of hard to believe," Josie agreed.

"She says Beau has been bruised, his clothes have been torn, and he has a dangerous cut near his eye."

"I know," Josie said.

"What I don't understand," her mother said, "is *why*? Why would you harm your oldest and best friend in the world?" Her voice was becoming louder. "What has he ever done to deserve such treatment?"

"Nothing," Josie said.

"Then there's Paula," her mother went on. "Paula Finch is my closest friend, as you well know. How do you imagine it felt for me to have to stand there and hear her tell me that my own daughter has become a bully? Paula is *very* upset. She started to lecture me on how I should be raising you, and when I tried to say something, she just cut me off!" Sandy Pucinski's voice had become shrill. "I felt so ashamed. Humiliated, really. And Paula was so cold! I don't know if our friendship will ever be the same."

Sandy Pucinski held the palms of her hands to her temples. Her headache was not improving, Josie could tell.

"What makes it worse, as Paula points out, is that you're so much bigger than Beau now. It's not even a fair fight."

"Oh no," Josie murmured. "I never thought of that."

"Well, you should have," her mother said. "You should have thought of several things before now. But as you didn't, you'll have your chance now. I want you to go to your room until your father gets home. Then we'll talk this over and decide what to do next."

Josie hung her head and turned to leave the room.

"*Josie!*" her mother screamed. "What in the world have you done to your hands?"

"Oh," Josie said. "They're just false fingernails. Don't worry, they'll come right off."

"I should hope so! Honestly, Josie, I don't know what to make of you anymore. You've changed so much lately I hardly think I know you. If this is a sample of what you're going to be like as a teenager . . ." Her voice trailed off, and Josie thought she saw her shudder.

Josie sat in her room and waited. She didn't know what was apt to happen next, but she was pretty sure it wasn't going to be pleasant.

One thing was true: her mother really didn't know her anymore. If she did, she'd have said, "Paula Finch has told me the most amazing story, but I know it can't be true." Or "Paula says you've been beating up Beau, but I know you would never do anything like that." Or even, "Why don't you tell me what *really* happened, Josie?" But her mother had said none of

131

these things. She had assumed that Josie was guilty without even asking to hear her side.

It made Josie angry. Or part of her felt angry. The other part felt guilty. It hadn't occurred to her that Paula Finch would complain to Josie's mother about her. It *should* have occurred to her—*would* have occurred to her, most likely, if the story had been true. But Josie hadn't thought of real consequences for a made-up story.

"Dumb," she said aloud. "Very, very dumb, Josie Pucinski."

And now Paula was upset with Josie's mother as well. That was perhaps the worst of all. How many times had she heard her mother rave about how much she loved Paula Finch, how wonderful it was to have such a good friend living so close by, how "irreplaceable" Paula was to her. Almost like a sister was what she always said.

Now Paula had been angry enough to be rude to Josie's mother. That was probably some kind of first.

The more Josie thought it over, the more she realized that this changed things in an important way. It was understandable that Paula would be angry at Josie for what she had allegedly done to Beau. Josie could accept that anger as being reasonable, and probably her just desserts for concocting a story.

And it was even sort of okay for Josie to accept her parents' anger on the same grounds. After all, what should she expect them to do, applaud?

But it was quite different to be the person responsible for spoiling her mother's and Paula's friendship. That was definitely *not* okay.

Kim stuck her head in Josie's room. "Psssst. Dad is home, and they're in the kitchen planning a hanging. I tried to help, but I don't know that it did any good. If I were you, I'd throw myself on their mercy."

"Thanks, Kim." Josie sighed. At least Kim didn't hate her . . . yet.

The minutes ticked by while Josie thought. She had to do something. The idea had been to help Beau, but instead she had just made a botch of everything. The trouble was, the only way out was to make a clean breast of the whole business, but then Beau would be back in trouble. The way things were shaping up, he would probably be in worse trouble than ever—all because of Josie and her big fat idea.

Josie pondered it, over and over. She had to tell the truth, but telling the truth would wreck things for Beau. Josie felt as though she were chasing herself around in circles.

Finally her father came in, carrying a tray of food. He set it on Josie's desk.

"I'm afraid you'll have to eat in here tonight," he said.

"That's okay," Josie said. She avoided looking at her father.

"I said this to your mother, and I'll say it to you: I

just don't believe you're capable of the behavior that's been reported to me."

Josie wanted to say, "I'm not," but she pressed her lips together and remained silent.

"Kim tells me you've been upset with Beau because he's fallen in love with a skateboard. Is this true?"

"Well," Josie said, "yes. But . . ."

"Josie, that's no excuse for hitting someone."

"I know that," Josie said. Then she thought of a question. "Dad, what *would* be an excuse for hitting someone?"

"Hmmm," her father said. "The answer to that question probably depends on who you are. Some people think you don't need an excuse at all, and other people think there is never an adequate excuse."

"What do *you* think?" Josie asked.

"Well, I happen to believe that it's permissible to hit someone if that's the only way you can protect yourself. But the idea is to use the minimum force to do the job. It's a matter of self-defense sometimes, Josie."

"That's what I believe, too," Josie said. She hadn't known it until her father said it, but that was just what she believed.

"Have you been hitting Beau in self-defense? Is that what you're trying to tell me?"

"No," Josie said.

"Well then," her father said, "in that case there is no excuse. So what I need to know now is whether we can count on you not to hit Beau in the future."

Josie thought of Matt Ventura. She wanted to say yes to her father, but it was Matt Ventura who needed to be counted on, and there was no telling what he might do.

"Then, as much as I hate to do this, you're grounded for the duration. Until you can give us your word of honor that you will not hit Beau again, you will have to stay home. No excursions, no bike rides in the park, no swimming lessons, and above all no going up to the Finches' flat. I know it's harsh, but this is a subject your mother and I feel very strongly about. Do you understand that, Josie?"

"Yes," Josie said.

Her father stopped in the doorway on the way out. "I still find the whole thing incredible," he said.

That's because it is, Josie thought.

Josie sat at her desk and stuck a fingernail in the mashed potatoes on her plate. I guess this is what jail is like, she thought. Even the mashed potatoes fit. They looked just like something you'd get in jail.

She licked the potato off her fingernail, then shoved the plate away. Then she studied her fingernails again from arm's length. They certainly were bright. She decided to keep them for a while. Right now they were the most cheerful thing in her life.

Chapter Twelve

When her parents had gone to work the next morning, and Kim had gone to the Conservatory, Josie wandered around the flat looking in all the empty rooms. It really wasn't *much* different, she told herself, from any other day of the summer. There had been lots of times when she was in the flat alone. And the way things had been with Beau and Matt Ventura lately, Josie had hardly gone anywhere except to her swimming lessons anyhow.

And of course she had quit the swimming lessons all by herself before she got grounded, so she wouldn't be going to them in any case. So how was this any different? It wasn't, she decided. This was just a normal day at home in the summer. Alone.

The only trouble was that she had to keep telling herself the same thing over and over. "This is just a normal day." For something that was supposed to be so normal, it sure was costing a lot of effort.

Late in the morning Josie went down to the garage

and rounded up some empty boxes. She took them to her room and began sorting things into them. One box she nearly filled with books she had lost interest in, everything from old picture books to nearly new copies of *Sweet Valley High*. A few favorites she left on the shelves. She would never part with *The Secret Garden*, of course, nor *Goodnight Moon*, *Charlotte's Web*, nor the copy of *The Call of the Wild* that still had her father's name in the front. But she weeded out an entire boxful. The Green Apple bookstore might buy some of them—if Josie ever got out of the house again.

"This is just a normal day," she said to herself.

Josie listened for Beau's footsteps in the room above hers but didn't hear anything. Every now and then she thought she heard a footstep, but then it would be quiet. She couldn't tell if he was up there or not. It would be nice if he would come down and ring her doorbell. Without standing sentinel at the living room window, Josie couldn't tell whether Paula was home or not, so she couldn't chance ringing the Finches' doorbell.

Josie filled another box with outgrown clothes and one with board games. Then she took a long, flat box and carefully laid all of her dolls in it. Her fingernails kept slowing her down, and one tore off as she folded a box top.

By midafternoon, Josie's room was transformed. It looked nearly spacious. All of the surfaces were

137

clear except for a few cherished items. It was a clean room—almost like Kim's.

I would have done this anyway, Josie thought. I've been planning to. It's not just because I'm bored to death, absolutely desperate, and in jail. I've been planning this.

Josie carried the boxes down to the garage, except for the box with the dolls. She slid that one under her bed. Then she stood in the center of the room and surveyed her surroundings. It looked wonderful. Her mother would be thrilled. Well . . . in other circumstances her mother would be thrilled. But Josie doubted that a clean room would make up to her mother for losing her best friend. It didn't for Josie.

She looked out the window. The clothespin swayed gently in the afternoon breeze. It was empty. She wished Beau would send her a note. She wanted to talk to him. If only she could dangle a note up. . . . If she told him what had happened, maybe he would decide they should tell the truth.

Kim came in when she got home from the Conservatory. "Wow," she said, "this place looks fabulous."

"Thanks," Josie said. "But I don't think it changes anything. I think Mom and Dad would still like to trade me in for another kid."

"Well, a clean room can't hurt," Kim said. "Tell you what—I have an old poster of Sting I've never hung up. I'll give it to you if you like."

Josie didn't care much one way or another about Sting. But she cared a lot that Kim was willing to give her the poster. She wouldn't give it to Josie unless she thought Josie was old enough to take good care of it. She felt as though Kim were treating her as a friend, rather than just a little sister. "Gosh, thanks, Kim," she said.

Josie was uncertain of the rules for being grounded. Did she have to stay in her room while her parents were home? Or did she only have to stay in the house? She decided it was safer to stay in her room until she knew for sure.

At five her father came to the doorway. Josie was lying on her back on the bed, studying her hands. Another fingernail had pulled loose. It flapped as she waved her hand.

"Hi, kiddo," her father said.

"Hi, Dad." Josie sat up.

"This room looks good."

"Thanks."

"Those fingernails, though—well, they're really some fingernails."

"I know," Josie said. "I haven't decided whether to keep them. I don't even know if I like them. And this one's loose." She flapped it at her father.

"Just don't try to sell it to me when it comes off," Bill Pucinski said.

Josie laughed.

"You're invited to eat in the dining room with us

tonight," her father said. "But you should understand that your mother is still quite upset."

Josie knew. This morning the only thing her mother had said as she left for work was, "I'm leaving. Remember you're grounded." She wished her mother would come see her room.

"Dad," Josie said, "what would you do if you had tried to help somebody, but you had just made a big mess instead?"

"I don't know that I can answer that, Josie, without knowing what you're talking about."

"Well . . ." Josie took a deep breath. "Suppose you had told a lie. But suppose that, at the time, you didn't think of it as a lie. Suppose you just thought of it as a plan to help this person—a person who really deserved the help. But then, suppose that everyone got really mad at you because they believed the lie."

"Hmmm. I don't know, Josie. That's a lot of supposes. But telling a lie is usually a bad idea, even if the intention is good. If you think about it, usually you can find a way to deal with things honestly."

"I couldn't," Josie said.

Her father didn't say anything.

"At least, I couldn't find a way at the time," Josie said.

"Can you now?"

"I don't know. But that's not the worst thing," Josie said. "The worst thing is that some other people got mad at each other because of the lie. Only they don't know about the lie, so they don't know that there's no reason to be mad. At least about that."

"This sounds extremely complicated, Josie, and I'm not sure I'm following you. Offhand, though, I think it sounds like the whole thing was a mistake."

"I think you're right," Josie said.

"Do you want to talk about it?" her father asked.

"No. At least not yet."

Bill Pucinski raised an eyebrow. "This wouldn't have anything to do with Beau, would it?"

This time Josie didn't answer.

"Well, okay. Think about it a little longer if you like. But remember I'm here to help if you need it."

"Thanks, Dad," Josie said. "But I might not need it. I think I know what I have to do."

When her father left, Josie opened the second drawer of her desk and got out a piece of binder paper. She sat at her desk and began to write.

> Dear Beau,
> Everything has gone wrong. I think we should tell the truth now, but I wanted to let you know first. Are you mad?
>
> —Josie

She folded the note in half, opened the window, and clipped it on the clothespin. Then she went in to dinner.

Dinner was strained. Hardly anyone spoke except Kim, who talked so much she hardly ate any food.

Mostly she talked about Keith and Yo-Yo Ma and what her chances were of getting into Juilliard School of Music. Josie couldn't tell whether Kim was glad of the chance for a monologue, or if she just couldn't stand the silence.

At bedtime Josie's note still hung on the clothespin outside her window. The fog was beginning to take a toll on it. The corners sagged, and when Josie turned out the light, it hovered like a ghost outside her window.

Alone in the flat again the next morning, Josie had a moment when she actually wished she were back swimming laps with Dumb Don. At least it would be something different to do. She regretted having worked so hard to clean her room. She should have made the job last two or three days.

Several times Josie distinctly heard Beau's footsteps in the room above hers. But the note on the clothespin flapped uselessly outside Josie's window. If only there was a way for Josie to signal Beau that she had written him a message.

Josie heard Beau's footsteps overhead again. That was it—a signal. Something to get Beau's attention. Josie raced to the front of the flat, through the dining room and kitchen to the utility room. She grabbed the broom and raced back to her room. Then she banged three times on the ceiling and waited.

Nothing. She couldn't even hear Beau walking around now. In a minute she tried again. Still nothing.

Then she tried once more. Silence. He must have gone to another room or even out to walk Mrs. Sloane's dog.

Josie's need to talk to Beau grew more urgent by the minute. If only she knew whether Paula was home or not, she might chance ringing the doorbell.

She went to the kitchen telephone. It was impossible to punch the buttons with her long fingernails, so Josie got a wooden spoon from the dish drainer and used the handle.

"Hello?" came Paula's voice on the phone. Josie quickly hung up. Paula hadn't sounded angry, but then she didn't know who was calling.

Josie sat on the couch and practiced disguising her voice. She tried a high-pitched squeak, then a low growl. "Hello, may I please speak to Beau Finch?" It sounded good to Josie. But was it good enough? Once Josie had phoned her mother at work and had spoken to her in a squeaky voice. She had even used a Southern accent. But the first thing her mother had said was, "Tell me why you're calling, Josie. I'm very busy here." Paula Finch knew Josie's voice almost as well as her own mother did.

Josie went back to her bedroom again and checked on the note. It was still there. She picked up the broom and banged on the ceiling again. Then she listened very intently, trying to detect any sound of Beau. When the doorbell rang, Josie nearly jumped out of her skin.

Beau stood on the doorstep. He was sporting a fresh bruise on his cheekbone.

"Oh, Beau," Josie said. She sagged against the doorjamb.

Beau walked in. "I need to talk to you," he said.

"And I need to talk to you," Josie said. "Now more than ever," she added, eyeing his cheekbone.

"Josie, I really appreciate how you've been helping me with the skateboard and my mother and all that."

"Yeah, well Beau . . ."

"And it was a good idea, Josie. A really good idea."

Josie cringed. "Uh, Beau . . ."

"Just hold on a minute," he said, "because I really need to explain this to you. See, I told my mother the truth this morning, and I don't want you to be mad about it."

"You *told*?" Josie couldn't believe it.

"Yeah, but Josie, I had a really good reason. See, even though your idea was good, it wasn't . . . well, it wasn't brilliant."

"You're telling me," Josie muttered.

"My mother stopped being mad at me, but then she started being mad at other people. First you, and now, believe it or not, she's mad at your mother. It seems like all the wrong people have been getting in trouble."

"There's been a lot of that going around," Josie admitted.

"So the first thing I decided was that Matt Ventura

144

was the person who should be in trouble. I had this idea that I would go to his house and tell his parents what was going on, so maybe they'd get him to stop. I thought my dad would think that was the right thing to do. I've been thinking about my dad a lot lately, Josie.

"The only problem was that I never got to see Ventura's parents—if he has any. He told me he was an orphan and lived alone, and then he jumped me."

"Kids don't live alone," Josie pointed out.

"I know that," Beau said. "But anyway, when I got home, I had this new problem." He pointed to his cheekbone. "My mother hit the roof and started ranting about you, and then I told her the truth. I didn't even really think about it, Josie. I just did it. But as soon as I did it, I knew it was the right thing to do—which I suppose is the reason it came out of my mouth without my thinking about it."

"Oh, Beau . . ." Josie felt limp with gratitude and relief. "Would you like a cookie?"

"Sure!" Beau said. He followed her into the kitchen.

Josie got a tall stool and reached into a high cupboard where she knew her mother kept the really good cookies—the ones with chocolate. Fig bars just didn't seem good enough for Beau.

She poured them each a glass of milk, and they stood at the counter, eating cookies from the bag.

"So you're not mad at me?" Beau asked.

"No way," Josie said. "See, I decided my little scheme was a great big mistake. That's what I wanted to talk to you about. I think I'm going to have to get a lot better at plots if I'm going to be a decent criminal. I don't seem to be naturally talented at crime —among other things."

Beau helped himself to a third cookie. "Well, you're talented at one thing, Josie: being a friend."

Josie was startled. Had Beau actually complimented her? He had the cookie split open in his hands and was licking the filling from the middle. He didn't seem to think he'd done anything unusual.

Still, maybe he did think she was someone special after all. Maybe when he got older and lost interest in skateboards, he would ask her to an R-rated movie.

His skateboard . . . He hadn't even mentioned it!

"Beau, what about your skateboard?" Josie asked.

"I don't know," Beau said. "Mom says she needs to rethink everything, whatever that means. So I don't know if she'll help me get it or not. But I don't think I could have enjoyed that skateboard, Josie, if everyone in the world was mad at each other because of it."

"I guess I know what you mean," Josie said.

Beau shrugged. "Anyway, I already own the deck. I think I'll go over to Skeet's Skates tomorrow and pick it up. It won't have any wheels or trucks, but at least I can keep it in my room and look at it."

"And plan," Josie said. Beau would spend hours

with his deck and *Thrasher* magazine. Josie could just see it.

"Yeah. And maybe when my dad gets back . . . well, we'll see."

Josie took another cookie. She couldn't remember when a cookie had tasted so good. It tasted of relief. And freedom. She wondered how soon she could be un-grounded. Today, maybe, if she left her parents a note: *I promise never to hit Beau Finch for the rest of my life.* That should do it.

"So, do you want to do something now?" she asked. "Like play cards? I was thinking we could learn to play gin rummy. It only takes two people. Or some other game. Just don't suggest Trivial Pursuit. I don't think I'm ready for that yet."

"To tell you the truth, Josie, I'm sick of cards, too. I was thinking it might be fun to go to the playground at Golden Gate Park. If we stopped down at the Seventeenth Avenue Market first, maybe we could get one of those cartons that has a waxy finish, and I could cut us each a piece to use on the slides."

"All right!" Josie said. Two long, curving, concrete slides wound side by side down a hillside at the Golden Gate Park playground. They were perfect for races, and you could double your speed on waxy cardboard.

Then Josie remembered. "What about Matt Ventura?" she asked. "What if we run into him there? It would be just your luck . . ."

"Oh," Beau said, "I didn't tell you that part yet. It was so weird, Josie. . . .

"I mean, here I was, trying to find a way to get Ventura to lay off—a way that my parents would maybe approve of—and instead he jumps me, and I'm about to end up a bloody pulp again. It made me so mad, I think I went half crazy. I started slugging him with all my might.

"Then, the next thing I knew, he was down on the sidewalk and I was on top of him. I was pounding him in the sides. He wasn't even hitting back anymore. He was just trying to fend me off. I remember seeing his nose, and for a split second the only thing I wanted in the whole world was to smash that nose flat. I had my fist clenched and a clear shot at him, and then . . . I don't know . . . suddenly I just didn't want to hit him anymore.

"It was the strangest thing, Josie. This was my big chance, and I could tell by his expression he knew he'd had it. But I just couldn't do it. I got off him and walked away."

Josie stood wide-eyed, clutching the front of her shirt. She had the sensation of not having breathed for several seconds. And what was it about Beau? He looked different to her somehow. Was he taller? It was hard to tell.

Beau walked to the sink and brushed the crumbs off his hands. "You're going to rip the front of that shirt with those fingernails, Josie."

"Oh," Josie said, startled.

"Besides that," he said, "they're really sort of ugly, if you don't mind my saying so."

Josie looked down at her hands. Suddenly the fingernails seemed garish to her. Why hadn't she noticed before? "You're right," she said. "In fact, I was just about to take them off."

Chapter Thirteen

Josie leaned against a utility pole at the end of her block and scanned the horizon for Beau. Where was he, anyhow? She shivered. The fog was blowing in fast, and her hair was wet from swimming.

Josie recalled with a certain amount of wonder the day in early August when she and Beau had walked back into Rossi Pool, stopped at the booth, and asked to speak to the director. Josie had been nervous, even though her father had assured her she had a right, almost an obligation, to complain about her lessons.

"We want to be in Cathy's class," Josie had said.

The director shuffled through some papers and pulled out a list. "I'm sorry, that class is full," he said. "We have a couple of openings in Don's class, though."

"Don's dumb," Josie said.

Beau elbowed her in the side. "Those are our places," he said, "and we don't want them. Don's a lousy teacher, and we weren't learning anything in his class. We want to be in Cathy's class."

"I'm sorry," the man said, "but class assignments are made on a space-available basis, and there's no space in Cathy's class."

"Let me get something straight," Josie said. "The city runs this pool, right?"

"Right," the man said.

"Then the city runs the lessons too, right?" Beau asked.

"Right again," the man said.

"And the mayor runs the city, right?" Josie asked.

"Well, yes . . ."

"So the mayor is really in charge of these lessons," Beau said.

"Well . . . in a manner of speaking," the man said.

Josie took a deep breath. "Then maybe we should ask the mayor whether the kids of this city are entitled to have competent swimming teachers," she said. She had rehearsed this last part and thought it sounded very persuasive.

"Hmmm . . ." the man said. "I see your point." He shuffled through some more papers, then said, "Wait here, I'll see what I can do."

When he returned a few minutes later, he said, "Cathy tells me she would be happy to take any kids who are serious about learning to swim."

"That's us!" Beau said. He turned to Josie and winked.

With Cathy they had learned to tread water, and once they had both qualified for the deep end of the pool, recreational swim time in the afternoons had become a favorite activity. Today was their last day; school would open tomorrow.

Josie looked up the street again for Beau. Ah, there he was. He seemed to be gliding toward her from the distance. Then, as he mounted the curb a block away, he lurched to one side. His skateboard flew off in the other direction.

"I still haven't mastered curbs," he said as he rolled up to Josie.

"So I noticed," Josie said. "Or speed either. The bus got me here ten minutes before you."

"That's not the point," Beau said. "Watch this." He took off down the block, zigzagging like a skier on a slalom run. Then he turned, got a racing start, and coasted all the way back to Josie, standing erect and looking almost smug.

"Do you want to try?" he asked.

"Not yet," Josie said. It was what she always said. But she had the idea that some day soon she might.

They turned onto 16th Avenue, toward home, Beau coasting slowly beside Josie. "I'm really glad you got that skateboard," Josie said. She meant it. Beau's happiness over his skateboard was irresistible.

"Yeah, after the dust settled," Beau laughed.

"Ugh. Don't remind me," Josie said. "The only part of that big two-family conference I liked was when my dad said, 'I knew Josie wouldn't hit Beau!' like he'd just won a jackpot or something."

"And the only part I liked was when my mother said she realized she hadn't been too understanding.

152

That was the understatement of the year." Beau did a one-eighty on his board, then pitched onto the sidewalk.

"I don't know whether you've noticed, Beau, but your deck is getting all banged up."

"It's supposed to," Beau said. "Skateboards aren't cool until they look well used."

Josie shook her head. Was this the same person who was wiping fingerprints off the deck two months ago?

When they reached their front steps, Beau picked up the board and began inspecting the trucks. Then he spun each Day-Glo green wheel once and watched as it gradually slowed to a stop.

"Josie," he said. "Do you remember when I told you that I used to be in love with you back in third grade?"

"Yes," Josie said. She did. Vividly.

"Well . . . I didn't exactly tell you the whole truth," Beau said.

"Oh, no," Josie said. She could feel it coming: he was going to take it back.

"The truth is I was in love with you in fourth grade too," he said.

Josie blinked.

"And in fifth grade too," he said.

"Oh!"

"But of course I'm not anymore," he added quickly. Beau's cheeks were red.

Josie smiled. "Of course not," she said. "I know that."